THE
MOURNE
MOUNTAIN
MURDERS

Totally gripping crime fiction

ROBERT McCRACKEN

THE BOOK FOLKS

Published by The Book Folks

London, 2022

ISBN 978-1-80462-046-5

www.thebookfolks.com

"Nobody gets justice. People only get good luck or bad luck."

Orson Welles

Prologue

When I was a wee girl, my daddy got shot. He didn't die, though. I used to sit for hours at his bedside as he slowly recovered. Sometimes I read to him, history books mainly, and at other times he used to tell me things. I didn't always understand what he meant.

One thing I remember him telling me was that in Belfast when someone gets shot the first thing that happens is that somebody gets the blame. It has always been this way. In a fractured society it's always one side or the other. But my daddy told me that once you get shot it no longer matters which side is to blame. A bullet does the same damage no matter who fired the gun. Motive means sod all to a corpse, he told me.

One day after he managed to sit up in bed for the first time, he told me that when he was well again, he would fight for justice for ordinary people no matter who they were or from which side of our divided country they came. I hadn't a clue what he was talking about, but I promised that when I was a grown-up, I would help him in whatever way I could.

Chapter 1

One of the Kardashians had moved into a new house. Six bathrooms, a health spa, a cinema, an indoor pool, and a restaurant-standard kitchen. Ursula flicked the page.

Another celebrity diet caught her interest. She could do with shedding a few pounds. She glanced from her magazine to the empty street then back to the magazine.

Sidney appeared from around the corner. He was running. Five feet nine inches, fifteen stone, late fifties: he didn't move well. Struggling and out of breath, he waved frantically to Ursula. But his daughter had her head down reading. Two youths were closing on him. He still had twenty yards to go until he reached his van.

At last Ursula looked up.

She started the van.

Sidney's face was puce as he climbed in.

'Go, go!' he shouted.

She pulled into the road as the first youth arrived with a baseball bat. He slammed it down on the bonnet. Ursula floored the accelerator but with her foot still on the clutch the engine roared, and the wheels spun. The second youth kicked at the driver's door.

'Ursula, drive the van!'

They shot forward as the baseball bat smashed through the rear window. One angry-faced youth kept pace with them for several yards. He mouthed obscenities and made gun signs with his hand. Ursula swung her door open. It smacked the youth in the face, and he went sprawling to the ground within the shadow of the peace wall. The irony would be lost on him.

'Are you all right, Daddy?' Ursula shouted as she pulled the door closed.

The second youth had given up on the chase. He stood on the road making rude hand gestures as his mate struggled to his feet, blood streaming from his nose. The van swerved to make the corner then gathered speed.

'Dead on,' Sidney eventually replied, wheezing heavily.

'Did you get it?'

'I think so.'

Sidney held his mobile in his hand.

'He was cleaning windows and, judging by his ability with that bloody baseball bat, I would say he was fit and able-bodied.'

'Our next call is up the Cregagh,' said Ursula, now driving at a more sedate pace from Madrid into Bryson Street.

'I think young Shane Taggart has taken it out of me.' Sidney panted. 'Let's go home. We can do the Cregagh tomorrow. I fancy a nice cup of tea and a Danish pastry.'

Ursula smiled sympathetically.

'I bought some fresh this morning,' she said.

'That's my girl.'

* * *

Their second-floor apartment on Kinnegar Road had an enviable view across the lough. Sidney spent his downtime on his recliner, a mug of tea in hand, pastries by his side, a book open on his lap, gazing towards Whiteabbey and Jordanstown. The vista was updated regularly by the coming and going of container ships and the Stena ferries from Belfast Harbour. Aeroplanes were well into their descent for George Best Belfast City Airport as they roared past his window. And there was always the turbulent weather. Lately, it had been cloudy with strong winds whipping up the water of the lough.

BB King played quietly on the CD player as Ursula examined her father's mobile phone. Usually, it was easy to find things on it. Sidney seldom used it except for business calls and occasionally the camera for his evidence gathering. Mobile apps and social media were anathema to her father.

'I can't find it,' she said from the breakfast bar. 'Are you sure you took the photo?'

'I got him perfectly. Up his ladder, cleaning away at a bedroom window.'

'Did you press the wee button to take the picture?'

Sidney didn't reply. Ursula knew rightly.

'And where is the one you got of him running with the baseball bat in his hand?'

'Should be there.'

'Ach, you didn't take that one either.'

'I was sure that I did like you told me. I wish I had my old camera. It was far easier to use.'

'But it's out of date by thirty years. Nobody uses a film camera nowadays. Everything is digital.'

'I'll just have to tell the DHSS what I saw.'

'That's no good, they'll want photographic evidence to present in court.'

'Then we'll go back tomorrow. I'm sure Taggart won't be put off window cleaning and claiming the dole at the same time by the likes of me.'

Sidney rested his head against the back of his chair. His mug was empty, and it was time for a doze.

Ursula sighed. Luckily, she had taken one picture with her phone. The image of an angry teenager slamming a baseball bat on the bonnet of her Vauxhall Combo might be enough to illustrate that Shane Taggart was doing the double. His claim to Social Security that he was unfit for work was false. She turned down the music. Her father was asleep.

Chapter 2

The morning was grey and cold. It was hard to say whether it would rain or if the wind would push the mass of cloud further north leaving the city in weak autumn sunshine. People in this part of the world endured rather than enjoyed the weather that greeted them on the doorstep each morning. He didn't care either way. It could rain all day, but it wouldn't stop him from getting out.

He put the rucksack into the boot of his car and set off from his parents' home. The boredom he'd suffered for more than a week was now unbearable. He'd found little to do around the house, his mind stuck in the mire. A walk in the mountains would clear his head. There he could think daft thoughts, talk aloud to himself and feel sorry for the mess he'd made of his life. When all the regret was swept away on a cool breeze, he could wallow in the solitude and the freedom it gave him to consider his next step. With a bit of luck, he would trample his way through life's bog and hopefully, at the other side, would not be faced with a great murky river to cross.

A red hatchback maintained a steady fifty at a discreet distance behind him as he headed south from Belfast, but he was oblivious to any threat that a car following might hold.

He was in sight of the mountains before he had made up his mind about where to begin his walk. Beyond the village of Dundrum, he turned right, moving away from the coast as the road climbed to the village of Bryansford, nestling by the edge of forest and mountain.

Three miles beyond the village, lay the Trassey Track, a popular hiking route into the heart of the Mournes. The trail ran alongside the Trassey River below the formidable crags of Spellack on Slieve Meelmore. He could recite the name of every peak, escarpment and valley rising before him – a knowledge gained when, as a teenager, he had spent his weekends rambling from one hill to another in rain, snow and the occasional heatwave. He gazed at the vast roundness of Slieve Meelmore, blunted by nature itself. Plumped beside it, like a gigantic spoonful of granite and heather, was the more ragged Slieve Bearnagh with its great tors of rock, brandished high in the skyline.

From the high road, he dropped to the left, taking the humped bridge over the river, and a few yards further on he pulled into a small, deserted car park, built to facilitate the mountain rambler. Seconds later, the red hatchback slid by, climbing the remainder of the hill, and rounding a bend. He had just closed the gate behind him at the bottom of the Trassey Track when the hatchback returned along the road. He paid it scant attention and set off on his walk.

* * *

'Are we not going after him?' Taggart asked. He looked bored and frustrated; his hands wedged in the pockets of his tight jeans. He kicked a stone across the tarmac and watched in delight as it bounced off the door of the other car. Shane Taggart was not cleaning windows today. He had a more lucrative job to do.

'Time enough,' his boss replied.

The boss lit a cigarette and leaned against the door of his car. Smoking was not a regular habit but this morning he was on edge.

'Can we trash his motor now?' said Quinn, wielding his baseball bat, swinging it wildly through the air.

'Don't be stupid!' Taggart scolded. 'It's supposed to look like an accident, you daft eejit. How's it going to look when the cops find his car's been wrecked?'

'Who are you calling an eejit?' Quinn snapped back. 'How would you like this rammed down your throat?'

He swung the bat in Taggart's direction.

'Pack it in!' their boss snapped. 'The pair of you will do as you're told, or it'll be more than yer man taking a fall.' He glanced at his watch. 'Another five minutes and we'll take up the scent. We'll have to keep our distance until we get to a place where we can do the business.'

'But what if we lose him?' Quinn asked.

His boss glared.

'It'll be your job to see we don't,' he said coldly.

Chapter 3

Ursula took a picture of a broken paving stone. Sidney remained in the van checking his notes to confirm that they had the correct location. He was still recovering from his exertions of the previous day. There were times when he attempted more than he was capable of at his age but running from men wielding baseball bats was not his normal or desired routine. Ursula, to her exasperation, was constantly reminding him to take things easier, but his old habits were not readily shrugged off.

A Mr Mark Forsyth had registered a claim for injury sustained when he'd tripped on the broken paving stone and hurt his back. The Northern Ireland Housing Executive were processing his case. Strangely, this was the fifth claim made by Forsyth in the last three years. Bizarrely, it was his second claim submitted with respect to injury sustained from tripping over a broken paving stone. When Sidney examined the paperwork, he noted that the paving stone from the earlier claim lay just thirty yards from the current one.

'Can I help you with something, love?' asked an elderly gentleman who was passing by. Slow on his feet, well muffled in a coat, scarf and cap, he carried a hessian shopping bag for life.

'I'm fine, thanks,' Ursula replied. 'Just taking a wee photo of the broken pavement.' She smiled at the man who had now stopped to watch.

'Plenty of those around here,' he said.

'Why do you think that is?'

'Drivers park their cars on the footpath and the weight cracks the slabs that haven't been laid properly. Then there's some people who deliberately break them so they can fake a trip over them and claim injury from the Housing Executive. But I didn't tell you that.'

Ursula smiled at the man's joke.

'You don't work for the Executive, do you?' he asked, suddenly concerned. 'Only, it's a nice wee earner for people round here.'

'What is?'

'Injury claims. Pays for new motors and holidays and the like. I'll leave you to it, love. Good luck with whatever it is you're doing.'

Ursula chuckled as she watched him tramp away. Sidney wound his window down.

'Don't be taking all day with that, Ursula. We've four more calls to make and we have to get the report done before tomorrow.'

'Nearly finished.'

She took one final photo, a white twelve-inch ruler placed next to the offending paving slab to provide some perspective.

Ursula drove the battered grey van to three more hotspots of broken paving slabs within housing estates in the east of the city. Each location was the subject of an injury claim either against the Housing Executive or the Department for Infrastructure.

The final call of the day, however, was an attempt to spot a known female entering a private house off the Malone Road. Their client was the woman's husband who was seeking information on his wife's clandestine activities when she was absent from the family home.

Sidney had already identified the house as belonging to a Belfast businessman known to be a bit of a lad, particularly with married women. All they needed was proof that Susan Crossley, forty-one and exceedingly glamorous, was going to the house twice a week for romantic liaisons with the man. A photo of Susan entering the house would be good. A photo of the pair in a loving embrace would surely be enough to satisfy their client Desmond Crossley.

'I'm bored with this,' said Ursula, yawning. They'd been waiting for a little over an hour. 'I'd love to walk right up to the front door, ring the bell, and when your man answers I'd ask him straight: Are you screwing Susan Crossley? It would save us all this bother.'

'I know, Ursula, but we have to be discreet. They mustn't know who we are or else they could take their anger out on us.'

'Like Shane Taggart did?'

'Exactly,' he said. 'Desmond Crossley is our client. All we have to do is confirm that his wife is having an affair. It's up to him how he deals with it. The other persons involved are not our concern.'

'I know. I just need something exciting to happen. Routine stuff like this gets me down at times.'

'It's our bread and butter, love.'

Frustrated after another two hours of waiting opposite the house and failing to see Mrs Crossley, Ursula was finally relieved to drive them home. On the way they bought their usual Wednesday meal, two fish suppers from the Fryer Tuck in Bloomfield. Father and daughter sat at the breakfast bar in their flat as they ate, watching the rush hour of planes arriving from Heathrow, Manchester, Birmingham, Glasgow and Edinburgh. This evening, John Lee Hooker provided the musical background. Sidney had a passion for the blues. Ursula had grown up with it. Music for the soul is how Sidney regarded it. It was a Belfast thing; blues music had always connected with its people. She couldn't argue and had never heard anything to rival or dispute Sidney's opinion.

When tea was finished, Sidney tidied up in the kitchen, while Ursula typed the various reports on the day's activities and emailed them to their clients. With no progress made in the Crossley case, their current workload was light, and she had the urge again to visit the house off the Malone Road to ask the owner if he was shagging another man's wife. But she realised that she was going through another period of boredom. Devoted to the business, Sidney Valentine Solutions, and to her father, she knew it wouldn't be long before something interesting came up.

It arrived sooner than Ursula had even hoped.

Chapter 4

The van was in the garage to be repaired. Ursula had walked the half mile to Holywood town centre to fetch the morning papers. She also bought some fruit scones from the home bakery in High Street. Sidney liked something tasty to start his day. They could do with cutting down on the luxuries, though. She wasn't overweight, certainly not fat, but on some days her jeans felt tighter than on others. As for her father, it was a futile battle to improve his eating habits. Sidney had few interests, but he did enjoy his food. If only his eating was matched by a desire for physical exercise.

Kinnegar Road had been cut off from the centre of town in the early seventies when the bypass was built. Ursula was too young to remember that, but it had resulted in no through-traffic on the Kinnegar side. There was also an underpass for pedestrians to avoid crossing the busy dual carriageway that linked Bangor with Belfast.

As she walked, Ursula arranged the day's forthcoming activities in her head. It didn't amount to much. They had no calls scheduled. Unless something came in this morning, they were left with stalking the Crossley woman. Matrimonial cases were not the most appealing to her or Sidney. But as her father said, it paid the bills.

A strengthening wind blew through her short brown hair as she emerged from the subway and strolled along the pavement below the esplanade. It blew off the cobwebs. She tried to scan the papers she'd bought from the newsagent next to the home bakery as she walked, but the breeze was too strong. From the morning edition of the *Belfast Telegraph*, however, she managed to read the headline and first paragraph. It quickened her stride to the point where she finally broke into a run to reach the flat.

Sidney was just getting out of bed as Ursula barged into his room. He wore pyjama bottoms but didn't always bother with a top and his tummy sagged over the waistband.

'See how that grabs you!'

'Ursula! I might have been stark naked.'

'Wouldn't bother me if you were. You need to look at this.' She handed him the newspaper.

Sidney was seldom rushed unless he was being chased by a youth wielding a baseball bat. He stood where he was, holding the paper, until his daughter took the hint.

'Right, I'm away, but you need to read that.'

* * *

Ten minutes later, Sidney sipped his tea while Ursula served him warm fruit scones, butter and jam. The front page of the *Belfast Telegraph* lay on the breakfast bar, the headline was the elephant in the room.

Identified. Man's body found in Mournes.

'What I can't understand, is what the hell was a wee glipe like Shane Taggart doing in the mountains?'

'A bit strange,' said Ursula, 'there can't be many windows that need cleaning.'

'But it hasn't said in the paper whether he was murdered or if he died from an accident. He didn't strike me as the mountaineering type.'

Ursula lifted her mobile and opened her local news app. Sidney continued browsing the paper.

'Police are treating the death as suspicious,' she read then added, 'We reported him to the DHSS for doing the double, and a week later he turns up dead. Seems a bit harsh for benefit fraud.' Her father had gone quiet. She knew he was thinking.

They finished their breakfast in silence. Sidney read the *Express* while Ursula took over the *Telegraph*.

'I suppose we should tell the police what we know of Taggart,' said Ursula. 'Just in case his benefit fraud had something to do with his death.'

Sidney looked up from his paper as if he'd been prodded awake.

'I wouldn't mind finding out what happened to the young lad myself.'

Ursula smiled with glee. That was her father all over.

'Oh shit!'

'What's wrong?' asked Sidney.

'The van is still at the garage.'

'Nothing wrong with catching a bus the odd time.'

* * *

They took a city-bound bus from High Street in Holywood and got off outside Strandtown police station in east Belfast. It was a modernised building of the PSNI but still maintained the bomb-proof walled perimeter from the days when the RUC were under threat from terrorists. Sidney was quite a regular visitor at the station, though not always welcome. His activities as one of the few private detectives in Northern Ireland at times tended to irritate those tasked with law enforcement.

'So, you reckon the DHSS have a shoot-to-kill policy for doing the double?' said the corporal with a snigger.

Neither Sidney nor Ursula even raised a smile. They had already done the jokes. Besides, DCI Ross Harvey was not a funny man. Not in that way. Sidney had always referred to him as "the corporal".

'That's about as important as he looks,' Sidney had once said. 'He acts like he has more authority than he has.'

Harvey was a hardened cop. He didn't handle public interference in police business very well. There were times though when he had needed the help of people like Sidney to solve those more puzzling cases, although he had always been happy to accept the plaudits. He sat in his high-back swivel chair in a cramped office looking unimpressed by the information coming his way. He had a small head on rounded shoulders, Brylcreemed black hair and a swarthy complexion with a five o'clock shadow.

Sidney was continually astounded by the man's poor memory. Harvey never seemed to recall that he and Sidney had gone to the same secondary school. It was Sidney's memories from that time which fed his dislike of the cop. A greasy toad who used to rile people was how he described the teenage Harvey. He was the type, Sidney frequently recounted, you always liked to see getting a hiding in the school playground. And here he was, decades later, a detective in east Belfast with no memory of Sidney Valentine.

'Taggart had a violent streak,' said Ursula.

'And how's that, love?' Harvey asked with glaring condescension.

Ursula had learned years ago not to be intimidated by the likes of the corporal. She merely smiled; her fresh face healthily illuminated. She noted also that Harvey's gaze was, as usual, sharply focussed on her large bosom. In her slight frame, her breasts were hard to miss – Harvey never seemed to have a problem.

'He took a baseball bat to our van,' she replied.

Harvey chuckled. 'Well, I doubt you'll get him to pay for the damage now.'

Sidney got to his feet. He'd already spent more than enough time in the company of the corporal.

'I just thought you should know about the benefit fraud,' he said. 'It might help with your inquiries.'

'Thanks anyway, Valentine. I'll pass it on to the guys in Newcastle. They're in charge of the investigation.'

Ursula rose from her chair and leaned across the cop's desk. She wore a sky-blue V-neck T-shirt beneath her open biker jacket. Harvey swallowed hard.

'How did Shane Taggart die? Are you treating it as murder?' she asked.

'I'm not sharing that information with the likes of you.'

Ursula swayed gently. Harvey had nowhere else to look.

'OK, he was shot. Now get out of my office and take that chest with you, love.'

Ursula giggled then winked at her father.

'Thanks, Corporal, it's always a pleasure,' said Sidney.

'Don't go poking your nose into this. I know what you're like, Valentine.'

Chapter 5

From Strandtown police station they walked for little over a mile heading to Mountpottinger Road, the district where, a week earlier, Sidney had observed Shane Taggart and his companion cleaning windows.

'Taggart's mate might still be working,' said Sidney.

'Well, I hope he doesn't come after us again with a baseball bat. We can't drive away this time.'

Ursula took her father's arm as they strolled down Albertbridge Road where modern housing developments had in recent years replaced the old dwellings of Belfast's industrial past.

An hour of searching for a window cleaner at work in the area proved fruitless. Sidney and Ursula therefore had two reasons for entering the Emerald Bar on Mountpottinger Road. Firstly, they sought information and secondly, they fancied a pint. At two o'clock on a weekday afternoon, there weren't many punters within. A couple of old boys sat over bottles of stout and were playing rummy. A man in his thirties leaned on the bar with a half-finished pint of lager in front of him. He and the youthful barman were glued to the racing from Worcester live on Channel 4. No one took them under their notice as Sidney stood at the bar waiting to be served.

'Two pints of Guinness, please,' he called to the barman who somehow managed to scrape his eyes from the racing.

The pints were served without chat, and Sidney joined Ursula at a small table next to the card players. It was not the most salubrious of pubs to enjoy a beer. Functional and taken for granted best described the tiled floor, worn faux-leather upholstery and the array of sporting occasions depicted on the walls, mostly of Gaelic games or of those heady days when Jack Charlton was manager of the Republic of Ireland football team.

'I can't believe what's happened to our Shane,' Ursula announced loud enough for all those present to hear.

Sidney glanced around surreptitiously for a reaction.

'What was he doing in the Mourne Mountains, that's what I would like to know?' she continued.

Sidney drank his beer, glad to have his thirst slaked.

'One day he's cleaning windows, the next he's dead. It's going to kill my ma when she hears,' said Ursula who at last paused to drink some of her pint.

On the TV a race had just finished, and a groan was heard from the man leaning on the bar. A few seconds later, though, he was towering over Sidney and Ursula. His jeans were washed out, his face bony, pock-marked and unfriendly. He held a glass in his hand, more as a potential weapon and less a container for what remained of his lager.

'You know Shane Taggart?' he accused more than asked.

His manner was threatening, pseudo-hard. But he didn't have the stature to match his bravado. An overly large brown leather jacket hung on him but did nothing to enhance his image. Neither Sidney nor Ursula felt intimidated.

'Aye, did you know him?' Sidney replied.

The man didn't answer but continued to study the strangers sat in his local. His eyes lacked any deep colour. He was tall but scrawny, his Adam's apple protruding from a long neck, and his sandy hair was in need of washing and trimming. He lacked any endearing qualities. A suspicious bully maybe, but he wouldn't make many friends that way.

'He was my cousin,' said Ursula with a teasing smile.

'Aye, I'm sure. What do you want?'

'I'm just looking to hire a window cleaner,' Sidney said with a smirk. 'Hard to come by round here.'

'Our Shane had a mate who worked with him,' said Ursula. 'Do you know where we might find him?'

The man's face cracked a bemused smile. He took a swig of beer and returned to the bar. His gaze focussed again on the television.

'I'd drink up and clear off if I were you,' he said without the need to look at them.

Sidney winked at his daughter. As they continued with their drinks, however, they noticed the barman slipping out of a door behind the bar. It was never a good sign. Ursula imagined a squad of hoods turning up and itching for a fight. It was time to go.

Emerging from the dim light of the bar five minutes later, they were relieved to find the barman alone, leaning against the wall and smoking a cigarette. There wasn't much to him — five and a half feet, and little meat on his bones. He had black straggly hair, his face pale and thin. Ursula smiled at him, and he acknowledged her with a flick of his head.

'Shane's mate has disappeared too,' he said, blowing out his smoke.

'Name?' Sidney asked.

'Terry Quinn.'

Chapter 6

The only information they had gleaned from the *Belfast Telegraph* about Shane Taggart's death was that his body had been discovered close to the Trassey Track. Sidney and Ursula had learned even less about the victim's background. They already knew from the DHSS file that Taggart had lived in the Short Strand. He was eighteen and had worked as a window cleaner while also claiming the dole. The question for Sidney was why a youth with apparently little going on in his life would venture into the mountains and end up dead.

The van rolled over a humped bridge and climbed the hill. Close to the start of the Trassey Track, they pulled off the road into the small car park. A strong wind blew up the Shimna Valley from the coast but today clouds were unusually absent from the County Down sky. Father and daughter were experienced hill walkers. Sidney had grown up with Scout hikes and bivouacking. He'd raised Ursula to appreciate the outdoors. Both were dressed for the conditions: hiking boots and windproof anoraks. Sidney donned a bobble hat. He didn't have much hair remaining and liked to have his ears protected from the cold.

They passed through a gateway and ventured onto the Trassey Track. It was easy-going at first, a gravel path with a gradual incline that ran between plantations of spruce and open moorland. Up ahead, however, as the track veered to the right and rose steeply, they saw a police Land

Rover and three officers chatting by a patch of grass. A few minutes later, father and daughter greeted the officers as a typical pair out for a day's hiking.

'How's it going, lads?' Sidney called out.

'Not bad,' one officer replied. 'You've picked a good day for it. It was chucking down yesterday.'

Two of the officers began rolling up police incident tape that had been stretched around an area about half the size of a football pitch.

'Is this the spot where that young lad was found?' Ursula asked.

'It is, aye,' said the officer.

'What happened?'

'Somebody shot him. Twice.'

'Any idea why?'

The constable shook his head.

'Can't say at the moment. I think the killer tried to make it look like suicide. They had placed the gun in the victim's hand. Assuming, of course, that it was the same gun that killed him. Forensics will confirm that. But you don't shoot yourself twice, once in the back and once in the head.'

'Had he been out hiking?' Sidney asked.

The officer shook his head again and smiled.

'I don't think so. He wasn't dressed as a hillwalker. Denim jacket, jeans and trainers are not what you would expect to see on someone venturing into the mountains. He was found by members of a rambling club. Probably been lying here for a day or more.'

The officer's colleagues were now waiting by their vehicle.

'Enjoy your walk, folks. I'm going for my tea break.'

Sidney and Ursula waited for the police to drive away then paced around the area that previously had been cordoned off.

'I'm sure the cops have licked the place clean,' said Sidney, nudging a tuft of grass with his boot.

Ursula gazed along the trail. 'I wonder what direction Taggart was coming from. Was he on his way into the mountains or was he heading out?'

'Could be that he was killed elsewhere, and his body was dumped here,' Sidney replied.

'But why here? Why not at the side of the main road instead of half a mile along the track. No need for that, surely?'

'Nothing much for us to see here unless you fancy going for a dander?' Sidney suggested.

Ursula shrugged.

'May as well make a day of it.'

Sidney plodded on with Ursula following. Without the stiff breeze it would have been a perfect day for walking in the hills. The Trassey Track led to the base of Hare's Gap, a saddle between two mountains. From there they moved upwards, pausing for a breather by the Mourne Wall. It was a favourite spot for hikers to rest before tackling a peak such as Slieve Bearnagh or strolling down to the shore of Ben Crom Reservoir. Sidney, however, was intent on going further. He fancied eating lunch on the huge dam that sat above Silent Valley. The lower slopes of Slieve Bearnagh fell steeply to meet Ben Crom Reservoir, but the land was rutted by several gullies where streams from the higher slopes had cut channels and fed the reservoir below.

Sidney and Ursula, however, would not get to enjoy their lunch. As they ascended a ridge, they spotted another pair of hillwalkers emerge from a gully and come towards them. The middle-aged man and woman seemed to be in a hurry, their speed increasing when they noticed Sidney and Ursula. When they drew within a few yards it was apparent that the woman was very distressed.

'There's a body over there,' the man said, breathing heavily. He pointed towards the slope that descended to the reservoir. 'We need to call the police,' he added.

He was dressed in hiking boots, breeches and a fleece jacket, and his face was flushed reddish purple from hurrying up the mountain. The similarly dressed woman looked pale.

'It is a young man,' she said her voice quivering, her whole body trembling. 'His leg has been broken but I think he has also been shot.' She burst into tears.

Ursula stepped forward and placed an arm around her shoulders.

'Where exactly?' asked Sidney.

The man removed from his rucksack a folded map, six inches to the mile scale, of the Mournes, and held it out. He placed his finger on the spot.

'Just beyond the entrance to that gully.' He gazed into the distance. 'About 300 yards from here.'

Sidney suggested that the couple sit down for a rest and await their return. Ursula was already bounding across the heathery slope.

As she entered the gully, her father beginning to slow and twenty yards behind her, she noticed what looked like a pile of old clothes lying in the brook. Negotiating a steep and slippery descent over moss-covered rock to the stream, she soon realised that it was more than a mere bundle of clothing. Then, from a few steps away, she called to her father.

'I think we may have found Terry Quinn!'

Chapter 7

'The woman was right. His leg has been broken,' Sidney said, standing over the body. 'And he's been shot.'

Ursula was already on her mobile to call the police, raising it in the air and moving around to get a better signal. Sidney examined the right leg of the man they assumed was Terry Quinn, his shin bone having pierced his skin and trousers. His blood had soaked the material and had been partially washed away by the stream. The left side of his head had a neat bullet hole just above his ear. A trail of dark blood had spilled onto the stones and trickled into the water, forming an horrific tributary.

Ursula gave their location to the emergency operator, while her father paced around the scene searching for anything that might help explain what had occurred in such a deserted and peaceful place.

'This guy was definitely not dressed for a hike,' said Ursula. The young man wore brown brogues and grey trousers, a blue shirt and a woollen cardigan. 'There's no wallet or phone on him. No ID. We can't be certain that it's Quinn.'

'So, was he killed first followed by Taggart?' said Sidney.

'Probably, if what that cop said is true about someone trying to make it look as though Taggart shot himself. Maybe the killer was trying to make it look as though Taggart shot Quinn then took his own life. Or was it the other way around; Quinn killed Taggart and then shot himself, his body tumbles down the gully and his leg gets broken?'

'But what were the pair of them doing way out here?'

Sidney wandered several yards from the body, hands in his pockets, seemingly taking in the view.

* * *

An hour later, seated on the heather with the man and his wife beside them, Sidney and Ursula watched as several police officers picked their way along the shoreline of the reservoir. It was slow-going because there were no distinct paths or trails in that area. Recovering the body to the reservoir's service road below the dam, where a Land Rover and several other vehicles had been parked, would be arduous.

Ursula had moved some distance from the dead body and she and Sidney ate ham sandwiches and shared their flask of tea with the couple at a spot overlooking the reservoir. As the police drew nearer, Ursula could see that they were accompanied by a mountain rescue team. It would be a while longer before anyone reached them.

Ursula sensed that her father was itching to be away. He had learned as much as he was going to from the scene and was eager to return to Belfast. They were merely waiting to pass on the crime scene to the police. Ursula knew better than to say too much. For instance, they would not mention to the police that the victim's name might be Terry Quinn. Identifying the dead man was their problem, Sidney told her. DCI Harvey had already warned them about getting involved in a police investigation. They realised, however, that news of their finding a body in the Mournes would eventually get back to the corporal.

It turned out to be the same group of police officers they had met earlier in the day. They were appreciative that Sidney and Ursula had alerted them to the discovery of another corpse in the mountains and had remained to help preserve the crime scene. A full police incident was declared, and by the time Sidney and Ursula were allowed to be on their way a posse of vehicles had arrived below Ben Crom Dam. More than twenty people, including detectives and forensics personnel, gathered at the scene.

Sidney and Ursula accompanied the couple back to the Hare's Gap then via the Trassey Track to the car park. Sidney didn't say much on the return hike. His pace had lifted and to carry on a conversation too would have left him breathless. The man thanked them as he helped his wife into their car. She was still shaken by the events.

Sidney listened to music on the forty-mile drive to Belfast. The blues helped him to think. He donned his dark sunglasses, reclined his seat, put his head back and soon had dozed off. Ursula nudged him awake again when she pulled up outside the Emerald Bar on Mountpottinger

Road. When they entered the pub in hiking clothes, they looked even more out of place than on their previous visit. The number of old men playing rummy had increased to four and two blokes propped up the bar. It was a busy afternoon. The skinny young barman acknowledged Ursula with another flick of his head. Ursula smiled and it was reciprocated.

'What can I get you?' he asked, his eyes on Ursula not Sidney.

She ordered two pints of Guinness.

'Yer man that was here yesterday,' Sidney began, 'do you know where we might find him?'

The barman looked suspiciously at Sidney but couldn't help returning his gaze to Ursula who beamed a cheerful smile for his benefit.

'He owns the chippy across the road.'

Then he watched as Ursula supped her pint.

'It's my night off,' he said, sounding unsure of himself, 'would you fancy going into town for a bite to eat?'

Ursula, trying to hold back a smirk, looked first at Sidney who was pretending not to hear the conversation then at the young barman, at least ten years younger than her. Bless. She was flattered.

'I can't tonight, love. I have my aikido class.'

'Right, no bother,' he said, his face flushing red.

She stifled her giggle as the youth found an excuse to move sheepishly to the other end of the bar.

'I think he has a wee fancy of you,' said Sidney.

'You think?'

When they had finished their drinks, Ursula called thanks to the barman, hopefully redeeming herself for causing him embarrassment. Outside, they crossed the road and fifty yards down stood outside a chip shop with the name on the sign above the window reading 'Sean's Suppers' and, in Irish, 'Suipéar Sean'. There were no customers inside but give it an hour and the queue would stretch out of the door onto the street. The not-so-friendly man who had confronted them in the bar the day before was preparing for the evening rush, dipping fillets of cod into a thick batter mix and then flash frying. He didn't speak when Sidney entered ahead of Ursula.

'Afternoon,' said Sidney. 'Need to ask you a few questions, Sean. I take it that's your name?'

'Says so on the sign,' he replied coldly, stealing a glance from his work to his visitors.

Ursula leaned both elbows on the counter.

'You seemed a bit unfriendly yesterday when we mentioned our cousin Shane,' she said.

'Who are the pair of you? I know you're not Shane's cousins. He doesn't have any cousins. Are you cops?'

Sidney eased his way behind the counter. Sean eyed him with suspicion.

'You're not allowed back here,' he said. 'Health and safety.'

'Na, we're not cops,' said Ursula. 'Just interested in what happened to Shane and his mate Terry Quinn.' She noted the lack of surprise on Sean's face when she mentioned Quinn's name.

'Somebody had a strong disliking of those lads,' said Sidney, 'we thought you might know who it was, Sean.'

'I don't know nothing! Even if I did, I wouldn't tell you two eejits. So, get the hell out of my shop.' He swiped a freshly battered cod fillet across Sidney's face.

'No need to be nasty,' said Sidney, clearing some batter from his left eye. He suddenly grabbed Sean by the lapels of his white overall and pressed him against the workbench.

Sean merely smirked. Clearly, it wasn't the first time he'd rubbed some guy up the wrong way or attacked him with a fillet of fish.

'Take your hands off me,' he said, 'that's assault.'

Ursula slipped behind the counter and in a series of swift movements took hold of Sean's right wrist, twisted it and pulled outwards so that his arm locked painfully at the elbow. Then she forced it downwards and dipped his hand in the tray of batter mix. The man yelped in pain.

'Now it's assault, Sean,' she said. 'Who you gonna call? Ghostbusters?'

Sean squirmed in pain.

'Once more, Sean,' Sidney whispered, 'who wanted Taggart and Quinn dead?'

'None of your business.'

Ursula, with a firm hold of the man's wrist, pulled his hand towards the fryer.

'Catch yourself on, love. You don't frighten me,' he said.

'Just messing with you.' Ursula grinned mischievously.

Then she twisted even harder on his wrist. Sean yelled in Sidney's face.

'I don't know nothing!' he cried.

Ursula applied more pressure to his wrist. 'Who would know, Sean?'

'OK, OK, Quinn's girlfriend!' he yelped.

This time Ursula maintained her hold on Sean's wrist. She wanted more information. She moved his hand closer to the sizzling oil in the fryer.

'I don't know anymore.'

There was no prospect of Ursula relenting. Sean's face was contorted with pain.

'Aagh! Stop, please! I don't know nothing.'

Sean buckled at the knees. Sidney nodded to his daughter, and she released the man's arm. Sean slumped downwards and became a sorry pile on the floor.

'Well, Sean?' said Sidney.

'Quinn's girl, Donna,' he gasped, caressing his throbbing wrist. Tears and snot dripped from his face.

'Where do we find her?'

'She lives over the river,' he grumbled. 'Friendly Street. Don't know the number. I swear!'

'Thank you, Sean. No need to make things difficult for yourself.'

'Piss off, the two of you.'

'Why don't you treat yourself to a wee fish supper?' Ursula jibed, dropping a raw fillet in his lap, and they left the irksome man cowering on the floor cradling his right arm.

Chapter 8

Sidney prepared the spaghetti bolognese to be ready for Ursula's return from aikido training. She attended the martial arts class once a week at the leisure centre on Marine Parade, opposite the railway station. This evening, Sidney sipped a glass of Bushmills as he worked, while music blared from the CD player. Outside, the water of the lough was incredibly still, disturbed only by the wake from a container ship leaving the harbour.

He turned from the cooker as two people entered the flat by the main door that led directly into the open-plan kitchen and lounge. Alongside Ursula was an unexpected caller, DCI Harvey.

'Look what I found, Daddy. Can I keep it?'

'No, love, I'm sorry, you have to throw the tiddlers back.'

'Hilarious, the pair of you,' said Harvey, marching through the kitchen into the lounge. 'What the hell is that racket?'

'Ach, Corporal, I didn't have you marked as a philistine as well as a dipstick.'

'You're all comedians in this part of the world.'

'So, what can I do for you?' Sidney asked as Ursula lowered the volume on the CD player.

Harvey, uninvited, dropped onto their brown leather sofa.

'I want to know what the pair of you are up to.'

Ursula shrugged innocently at Sidney, and he shrugged back.

'OK, enough of this bullshit. What were the two of you doing up the Mournes this morning?'

'Out for a walk, as you do,' said Ursula.

Harvey watched as she peeled off her sweatshirt and stood before him in a black sports vest and leggings. He tried hard to focus on Sidney but couldn't prevent his eyes from returning to her shapely figure.

'Newcastle station called me with your details after you two, apparently, just happened to stumble on a dead body. And lo and behold this body may be linked to the other dead body found nearby the other day. So, what are you not telling me, Valentine?' He watched as Ursula took a long drink from a glass, throwing her head back to savour the cool water.

'There's nothing to tell, Corporal,' Sidney replied. 'I've told you what I know about Shane Taggart. I don't know anything about the other bloke that we found.'

The detective shook his head in disgust or frustration, both most likely.

'Why do I not believe you two? And don't bother answering that. It's not worth hearing.'

Harvey got to his feet with a sigh and headed towards the door. He turned around and stabbed a finger in the air at father and daughter.

'Keep your nose out, Valentine. I know rightly you're up to something. And get some decent music to listen to.'

'I'll have to borrow your Nolan Sisters CDs, Corporal.'

'Stop calling me corporal.'

Sidney held the door open for the detective to stomp out. With a casual flick, he swung it closed behind him.

'Remind me again why we do this,' said Sidney a few minutes later, setting plates with spaghetti bolognese on the counter.

Ursula was choosing another CD.

'Justice, Daddy. It's your fight for justice. No matter what they had done those young lads deserve justice, and their families have the right to know what happened to their loved ones. The cops can't always get it for ordinary people, so you and I have to try. Why were two young lads shot in cold blood? Do you think maybe it was sectarian?'

'Always possible in this country, but it's more likely to be gang-related. That's what I want to find out, love.'

Chapter 9

Over the Albert Bridge, and into the markets area, Friendly Street had not always lived up to its name. There were times in the past when Sidney would not have felt safe venturing here. In Belfast it was always apparent where local sympathies lay. The markets area held reminders of the old conflict from the nationalist point of view with Irish flags and political murals interspersed with tributes to Glasgow Celtic. But times change and needs must. The markets area, like much of central Belfast, had undergone extensive redevelopment and Friendly Street now consisted of an array of modern, golden-brown brick terraces sweeping in a wide arc. On one side, the houses fronted the busy thoroughfare of East Bridge Street. Vehicle access was to the rear.

'There could be half a dozen Donnas living around here,' Ursula said as they cruised slowly in their van.

'We don't know if Terry Quinn even lived here with his girlfriend but, assuming he did,' said Sidney, 'we'll look out for a house with people coming and going from it. If word of Quinn's death has reached his girlfriend Donna, she may already have mourners calling at her home.'

'Including the cops.'

Ursula slowed the van thirty yards short of where two police vehicles were parked.

'We'll wait until they've gone,' said Sidney. 'No point in giving the corporal another excuse to give off.'

They remained in the van. It wasn't long before two uniformed officers stepped from a house in the middle of a row, got into one of the marked cars and quickly drove away. The second police vehicle soon followed.

The usual weather service had been restored after the hiatus of the previous day. A cold drizzle fell as Ursula left the van, approached the house where the police had just been and rang the doorbell. It was not long before the door was opened.

'Are you Donna?' she asked of a young woman with short black hair, a round face and tearful eyes. She had a stout figure and was dressed in black leggings, a baggy T-shirt and a long black cardigan.

'Aye, who are you?'

'I take it you were Terry's girlfriend?'

The woman burst into tears. Ursula stepped closer and gave her a hug. Just as well that Sidney had stayed in the van, he would have barged on with his questions without a thought for the poor woman.

'Terry never harmed anybody,' she sobbed. 'Who would do the like of this?'

'That's what I was going to ask you, Donna. Do you know if Terry was involved with someone who was capable of killing?'

Looking years older than her twenty-two, Donna wiped a sleeve across her face and shook her head slowly.

'No,' she whimpered. 'My Terry always stayed out of trouble. You still haven't told me who you are.'

'Shane was my cousin,' Ursula replied, seeing no harm in using the white lie once again. 'Did you know what Terry and Shane had been doing in the Mournes?'

Donna shook her head then accepted another hug from Ursula.

'Is there anyone else who hung about with Terry and our Shane?'

'Sean might know.'

'Is that Sean who owns the chippy on Mountpottinger?'

Donna nodded.

'Do you know where he lives?' Ursula asked. 'Only, I have a feeling he might be off work today.'

Donna looked surprised by the question.

'Next door,' she said.

Stepping outside, Donna crossed the shared driveway between her house and the adjacent one and knocked on the door. After a few seconds, a familiar face appeared behind the glass. On seeing it was Donna, Sean opened his door. It seemed that he hadn't noticed Ursula standing to the side.

'Hiya, Sean,' Ursula chirped. 'How's the wrist?'

Instantly, the man drew back revealing his heavily bandaged wrist. Ursula smiled gleefully on seeing the fear enveloping Sean's face.

'This is Shane's cousin,' said Donna. 'She wants to know if Terry and Shane were hanging about with anyone else?'

Sean made no reply. He glared angrily at the two women, then slammed his door.

'He's a bit odd,' said Donna. 'Doesn't like strangers. Would you like to come in for a cup of tea?'

'No thanks, love. I'm sure you have more than enough to do with family and friends calling to see you.'

'There's no one I know of who would want to harm my Terry,' said Donna, now with recovered composure. 'He was a lovely fella.'

'Somebody may have wanted it to look like Shane killed Terry and then shot himself.'

Donna cupped her hand to her mouth.

'Shane and Terry have been best mates since primary school. They would never have hurt each other.'

'Shane had been shot twice. It wasn't suicide, but it's not certain whether he killed your Terry.'

'How do you know all this?'

'I spoke to the policemen who recovered Shane's body.'

For a moment, the two women merely exchanged wilful stares, as if they both were trying to make up their minds about the other. Finally, Ursula thanked the woman and wished her well.

Sidney was attempting to browse the internet on his mobile when Ursula got back into the van. He tended to become frustrated sifting through a plethora of useless information when all he needed was access to a local news app for the latest about the two deaths in the Mournes.

'Nothing,' she said, looking pensive. She turned the key in the ignition. 'Although, surprise, surprise, that eejit Sean is her next-door neighbour.'

'That's convenient,' said Sidney. 'Or maybe it's just suspicious.'

Chapter 10

Deramore Park was an exclusive area off the Malone Road in the south of the city, a leafy district with expensive property. Many of the houses had electric gates, high walls and hedgerows. Sidney and Ursula could do little but sit in their van across the road hoping for the arrival of Susan Crossley for her afternoon love session with Martin Shiels. The house in question was a modern build made to look perfectly in step with the Edwardian red-bricks in the vicinity. Electric gates and a tiled driveway led up a slight incline to a huge structure with bay windows and a conservatory on the left side.

They'd only been there for a few minutes and already the pair were bored. Even the music had been switched off. They had another investigation of insurance fraud to pursue on behalf of the city's transport authority. But it would have to wait, while they watched for Susan Crossley.

'What do you know about Martin Shiels?' Ursula asked, breaking a period of silence between them.

'He is a man with a reputation. Aside from his philandering, his business activities are not exactly on the straight and narrow. His assets have been frozen more than once while the police investigated him. He's never been charged with anything, but the rumours still abound. The talk is that he is employed by criminal gangs spawned from paramilitaries and there is a link to organised crime in Scotland. Allegedly, he collects the proceeds from illicit activities, somehow washes it clean and takes his cut.'

'I'm sure he's not the only bloke round here who's in bed with paramilitaries. It's a hell of a dangerous occupation, though.'

A minute later, they observed the woman they assumed to be Susan Crossley stepping out of her silver Mercedes. She had driven through the electric gates and parked on the driveway close to the front door of the house. The gates had then swung closed behind her. She was dressed in business clothes, a dark tailored suit and high heels. Her auburn hair toppled off her shoulders and, despite the dull weather, expensive sunglasses rested on her head. She looked distinguished and accustomed to an opulent lifestyle. Ursula recorded the scene on her phone. At one point, the woman glanced cautiously behind her as she strode elegantly to the front door of the house.

'God, she's a honey all right,' said Sidney. 'Looks like one of them supermodels. What's she doing getting involved with a man like Martin Shiels? She's premier league and he's fourth division, Sunday morning kick-about.'

Ursula continued recording until the woman had opened the front door with a key and stepped inside. When the door closed, Ursula replayed the video for Sidney to watch.

'Pity we didn't get a shot of her in the arms of her lover-boy,' she said.

'This recording might be enough to convince the husband.'

'Hold on, what's up?' Ursula said with a start.

The door of the house had opened again, and the woman believed to be Susan Crossley dashed out. She ran to her car, its lights flashing as the doors unlocked. She jumped in and seconds later reversed down the drive crashing through the metal gates and spilling onto the road. The engine revved loudly, the wheels spun, and finally the car roared away at speed towards the main road.

'What the hell?' gasped Sidney.

He got out of the van in time to see the Mercedes in the distance rushing onto the Malone Road, angry drivers blaring their car horns at her failure to give way.

Ursula examined the buckled gates that now hung awkwardly on broken hinges. Sidney gazed at the house. He fully expected to witness someone rushing out in pursuit of Susan Crossley.

'Why is no one coming out to see this?' said Ursula.

Sidney was already on the driveway heading for the house. The solid oak door lay open. Ursula trotted after him.

'Hello?' Sidney called.

There was no response. He glanced at Ursula, who shrugged then intimated that they should venture inside.

All was quiet as they entered a lavish hall with light-coloured floor tiles and a staircase that swept around a curved wall to the first floor.

'Hello?' Sidney called again.

He looked at Ursula who ushered him further inside.

'Anyone here?' she called, opening a door to reveal a spacious but deserted lounge. Nothing seemed out of place, except for an empty whiskey tumbler resting on a coffee table.

Sidney quickly checked the other rooms on the ground floor. He found a huge kitchen with an adjoining dining area that gave onto the spacious conservatory affording views of a covered and furnished patio and beyond that a landscaped garden. Ursula discovered a TV lounge, better described as a home cinema with luxurious velour seating for eight, a large wall-mounted screen and a well-stocked bar. Sidney came across a bathroom and a study adorned with bookshelves, a solid-wood desk of dark wood, a photocopier and a laser printer.

'Not a soul,' he said, joining his daughter back in the hall. 'Let's try upstairs.'

They encountered six closed doors on the first floor, and Sidney hurried directly to what he guessed would be the master bedroom, the door of which lay wide open. Ursula followed him inside. The room was deserted but the duvet on the super-king-size bed lay unstraightened.

'Daddy!' Ursula called from the ensuite.

Chapter 11

Sidney stepped into the bathroom and stood beside his daughter.

'Would this be Martin Shiels?' said Ursula with a grave sigh.

The water in the jacuzzi was foaming red. It bubbled and frothed. The head of the man presumed to be Martin Shiels bobbed on the surface. The rest of him was only just attached to his head and lay stomach-down on the floor by the edge of the sunken tub. The dead man was huge and naked. Blood was spattered over the tiles and the steps leading to the jacuzzi. A picture window behind the tub allowed a sudden appearance of afternoon sun to highlight the gruesome scene. If one cared to look, there was a magnificent view of the extensive rear garden.

'If the Crossley woman didn't do this, she certainly got a shock when she saw it,' said Ursula. 'What do we do now?'

Sidney grimaced.

'We'll have another look around for anything to help us – paperwork, notebooks, links to the Crossleys – and then we'll get the hell out of here. I'm not hanging about to explain myself to the likes of DCI Harvey. Not when we have no idea what's going on.'

Hurriedly, they resumed a search of the house, Sidney finishing the upstairs and Ursula returning to the ground floor.

The other bedrooms were pristine and looked as though they were seldom used. The main bathroom appeared to be the same. All was sparkling clean and tidy. There seemed to be nothing of interest for Sidney to find. Returning to the master bedroom, he browsed the drawers of the bedside tables. He found some boxes of prescription drugs, penicillin and Viagra, pens, condoms, aftershave and a half-bottle of vodka. The built-in wardrobes were neatly lined with suits, trousers and shoes. Sidney checked the pockets of the jackets and then opened several cardboard boxes on the wardrobe floor. They contained sports trainers and golf shoes.

Downstairs, Ursula had not fared any better. She found several bills lying on the desk in the study. One was from a catering company for recent services provided at the home address. There were also two credit card statements. It appeared that Martin Shiels' outgoings for a single month ran to tens of thousands of pounds. Next to the desk was an office-standard Chubb safe. It sat waist-high, but Ursula found it to be locked. She didn't have time to figure out a way of getting it open. There was one locked drawer in the desk, but the two that were open held only stationery.

When she entered the extensive kitchen the sight of it induced a whistle from her, but the entire place hardly felt like a home. It had a clinical feel and lacked any personal touches. There was little food in the fridge or in the cupboards, although a wine rack and a glass-fronted cooling cabinet were well-stocked with bottles.

'Let's get out of here before the cops show up,' Sidney called from the entrance hall.

Ursula retreated from the kitchen and met her father by the front door.

'I found this lying on the bed.' He held up a black pocket diary. 'There might be something inside we can use.'

They left the front door ajar behind them and hurried back to their van. As Ursula drove them away, she recalled seeing a security camera high on the outside wall of the house. If it were operating, then the entire proceedings of them entering the house would have been recorded. No doubt the cops would come looking for them soon.

'Where to now?' Ursula asked.

'Let's see if Susan Crossley has made it home.'

Chapter 12

'What I'm surprised at,' said Sidney as Ursula negotiated the city traffic, 'is what on earth was a beautiful woman like Susan Crossley doing having an affair with Martin Shiels. He was ugly as sin and that's before somebody killed him.'

'Even her husband is not exactly an Adonis, and he's at least ten years older than she is,' said Ursula. 'Maybe Susan goes for something other than looks in her men.'

'There's hope for me then, but she's going to have to explain a bashed-up Mercedes to Desmond.'

'That's the least of her worries,' Ursula said. 'The police are going to know she's been at Shiels' house. There was CCTV at the property. And besides, we will have to tell her husband what we saw.'

The Crossley home nestled in the heart of Cultra on the North Down coast of Belfast Lough. It was arguably the most exclusive district in Northern Ireland. Property prices were high and always on the rise.

Ursula stopped the van by a grass verge in a leafy lane outside a sprawling Georgian-style building of grey stone surrounded by neat lawns and trimmed hedges. There were no cars visible on the sweeping concrete driveway.

'So, she hasn't made it home yet,' said Ursula.

'The gates are open. Maybe someone is home, and their car is parked around the back.'

Sidney got out of the van and strolled along the driveway. When he reached the white-painted front door, he pushed the button of the doorbell. It was a smart system. Within a couple of seconds, a voice spoke on the intercom. It was enough to confuse Sidney. More technology to be endured.

'Mr Valentine, I'm not home right now. If it's urgent you can come to the office.'

'Have you spoken with your wife this afternoon, Mr Crossley?'

'No, I haven't heard from her all day. In fact, the last time I saw her was yesterday morning. I've been in London on business.'

'In that case, we need to talk.'

'Come to the office. You have the address.'

They drove back to the city and Ursula waited on double-yellows, while Sidney went to the sixth floor of a modern block in Bedford Street, the head office for Crossley Imports Ltd. He entered a functional reception where the colour grey predominated and was greeted by a polite woman seated behind a semi-circular desk.

'I've come to see Mr Crossley.'

The woman, late-twenties, red-haired and wearing dark-framed glasses, smiled weakly and looked rather mystified. She did not immediately answer.

'He's expecting me,' said Sidney, tapping his fingers on the counter.

'Em, I'm afraid you've just missed him,' said Patricia, her name badge pinned to the lapel of her jacket.

'Do you know when he'll be back?'

Patricia shook her head doubtfully.

'Do you know where he has gone?'

'I'm afraid not. To tell you the truth, he seemed in a bit of a rush. You could try his mobile.'

Sidney remained in the reception while he attempted to reach Crossley by phone. It cut immediately to voicemail. He left his card with Patricia and asked her to call him when she next heard from her boss. When he reached the street, he found Ursula parked a few yards further along from where she had left him.

'We're losing more people than we're finding,' he said, settling into the van.

Chapter 13

Sidney sat by the large window in his flat leafing through the pocket diary he'd taken from the house on Deramore Park. Ursula read in a magazine about the latest celebrity plans to help penguins in Antarctica, while potatoes boiled in the pot on the stove.

Much of what was written in the diary was illegible. Assuming it had belonged to Shiels, the man had poor handwriting. Times and numbers were reasonably clear, but Sidney was unable to decipher names and other scribbled details.

'I wonder who or what is C? It's all over this diary, but I can't figure it out.'

'Let me have a look,' said Ursula. 'My eyesight is better than yours.'

Sidney tossed the diary to her.

'He was certainly a cautious man,' she said after a few minutes browsing. 'He never used full names for any person or any place. For instance, on Saturday, 13 February, C at E. So, C could be a person and E is a location.'

'Europa Hotel, maybe. Surely, it doesn't simply mean coffee at the Europa?'

'S followed by a tick. I wonder what that means? If C is a person, he or she gets mentioned a hell of a lot.'

Ursula continued to study the diary of Martin Shiels, while Sidney rescued the potatoes on the cooker. He continued preparing their dinner, frying sausages, mashing the potatoes and making onion gravy. When it was ready, they sat down together at the breakfast bar. Sidney poured two glasses of orange squash. All through their meal, Ursula studied the diary, jotting down notes when she believed she had deciphered some of the content.

'According to this, on Friday morning of this week at eleven o'clock there is something about 8K.'

'Doesn't help if we don't know the location,' said Sidney.

'I reckon it's Shaw's Bridge.'

'How do you figure that out?'

Sidney snatched the diary from Ursula and examined the entry.

'It just says SB,' he said. 'So, how certain are you that it means Shaw's Bridge?'

'I'm not one hundred percent,' Ursula replied, 'but there are several dates where SB is mentioned and once, on January 10, it just says bridge.'

'Worth going to have a look, I suppose,' Sidney mused. 'Otherwise, it's a dead end so far. Two lads associated with our benefits fraud investigation get shot and now our surveillance of Susan Crossley runs into the murder of her lover. Our cases aren't usually like this.'

'We have to speak with Susan Crossley; she is the link to Martin Shiels.'

'That might not be straightforward if the woman has run off or gone into hiding. Right now, we can't even talk to the husband.'

'I wonder what the police will make of it all?' said Ursula. 'Do you not think we should have reported it?'

'And incur the wrath of the corporal?' Sidney shook his head. 'We're staying out of this one.'

Ursula grinned disbelievingly.

'I can't wait to see who shows up at Shaw's Bridge,' she said, still grinning and knowing full well that she was baiting her father.

'It might be interesting,' Sidney replied, and Ursula knew then that they were definitely not staying out of this one.

After dinner, Ursula loaded the dishwasher, tidied around the kitchen then threw herself onto the sofa, her legs outstretched. Sidney had poured some whiskey and settled into his chair by the window. Blues music, however, was finished for this evening. Ursula was now watching *Coronation Street*.

Neither father nor daughter, despite their nonchalance, could dismiss the image of a man with his head partially blown off and floating in his jacuzzi. Ursula knew well that between his dozing, her father was thinking of the next steps in their investigation of two fresh mysteries.

Chapter 14

The murder of Martin Shiels was big news. His friends expressed shock and lauded his many business achievements and philanthropic activities. His enemies, while condemning the despicable act of murder, did not fail to mention his dubious lifestyle and associations with criminality. This was a well-worn word in Northern Ireland when being careful not to point the finger at any specific section of the community. At times the political ramifications of finger pointing were regarded as a threat to the ongoing peace process. The PSNI issued a statement condemning the murder and saying that following the discovery of a body at a house in Deramore Park, a rigorous investigation was underway.

'That's police jargon for we haven't a baldy notion what's going on,' said Sidney as he ate his porridge doused in maple syrup.

'They haven't said that they're looking for a woman in connection with the murder,' said Ursula, still in her pyjamas and munching on toast. The diary belonging to Shiels lay open in front of her. 'What if C simply stands for Crossley?'

'Could be, although was Shiels not more likely to have written S for Susan? And if referring to the husband, maybe it would be D for Desmond.'

* * *

Twenty minutes later, Sidney emerged from his bedroom dressed in shirt and trousers, ready to go. Ursula was brushing her teeth when he stood at the open bathroom door.

'I need you to drive me to Cultra,' he said, putting on his anorak and a tweed cap. 'Maybe the Crossleys have made it home by now, although Desmond is still not answering his phone.'

Ursula always did the driving. Sidney hadn't driven for more than ten years. He had never felt comfortable on the road since the time when he'd been shot more than twenty years ago. Once Ursula had passed her driving test, he was happy for her to take the wheel.

It took less than ten minutes' drive from their flat to reach the impressive home of the Crossleys. Ursula stopped the van at the open gates, but Sidney gave her a look suggesting that on this occasion she should proceed all the way to the house rather than have her poor old father traipse up the drive. With a disgruntled sigh she drove on, stopping by the front door. She hurried from the van and pressed the bell.

'No answer from the doorbell thingy except for the automated greeting,' she said when she got back into the van.

'I've just called Crossley's office,' said Sidney. 'His secretary hasn't heard from him since he hurried off yesterday. It's time we had a look inside the Crossley homestead.'

Ursula drove the van around to the rear of the house, stopping in a spacious yard. A triple garage sat opposite the house and there was a large well-maintained garden beyond.

'This place is bound to be alarmed,' said Ursula.

'If they fled in a hurry, maybe they didn't have time to set it,' Sidney replied, peering through the kitchen window.

Ursula tried the handle on the back door then went to the conservatory at the side of the house. She found that the patio doors were also secure.

'Locked,' she said, just as Sidney poked his elbow through a small square pane of the kitchen door. After the tinkling of glass, he smiled contentedly at the silence.

'Brilliant, no alarm. Lucky for you,' said Ursula with an admiring smile for her father.

He wasted little time reaching his hand through the space, slipping the lock of the door and venturing inside. They stood in an expansive kitchen and dining room, with modern fittings but designed to give a country-cottage feel to the house. Sidney did not get the impression that anyone had departed in a hurry. The kitchen was clean and tidy, a mains switch indicator light was on for the dishwasher and a wall-mounted television was in standby mode. They wandered through the ground floor of the house. Stepping into a small lounge, Ursula noticed a laptop open and resting on the arm of a sofa. She sat down and switched it on.

'What does Susan do for a living?' she called to Sidney who, distracted, was studying the CD collection of classical music stored in a bookcase in a corner.

'She's an accountant and, according to Mr Crossley, she mainly works from home.'

'What's her date of birth?' Ursula was trying to access the laptop, but a PIN was required.

'No idea.'

Sidney sifted through some correspondence that was lying on a sideboard next to the disappointing music collection. Ursula had quickly abandoned her attempts to access the laptop.

'Well, well,' he said. 'Is it possible that Susan Crossley does not use her married name for her business? Here's a letter addressed to Susan Shiels.'

'That can't be right,' said Ursula. 'She'd been having an affair with Martin Shiels. Don't tell me they're related.'

'We never actually confirmed the affair,' Sidney replied.

Chapter 15

Rosie had not slept well. Instead, she spent the night flitting from one door to another, checking they were locked, keeping an eye on the normally quiet cul-de-sac. There was nothing left now that was worth staying in this house for. Her marriage was over. She realised that much. She must get away. And she had to go before he came for her. Connor slept soundly in his room, but Rosie knew the danger they were facing. She would do anything to protect her son.

Close to dawn, as she moved around the house, she gathered clothes for Connor and herself, packing them in suitcases and sports bags. There were ample funds in the current account, and she had some cash hidden in the wardrobe for emergencies. This was such an emergency. She'd decided that the time had come to finally get far away. Merely fleeing to her parents' house was not enough. They would not be safe in Andytown, only a couple of miles away. She knew that he would come for her there, and her parents would not be able to protect her. She and Connor had to get out of Belfast, to England or maybe further to France or Spain.

Her sister lived in Hampshire; perhaps for now it was her best bet. Staying with Claire in Basingstoke, she could make her money last until she got settled in a place of her own. She could only pray that he would not come after her. Surely, not all the way to Hampshire.

In the garage, she loaded the car with their belongings ready to go when daybreak came. It was a sad image seeing your whole life stuffed into a Ford Fiesta. Her clothes and

Connor's, his favourite toys, and several of her books and treasured photographs filled the boot.

Seated at the kitchen table, a mug of strong coffee beside her, she used her phone to book a place on the morning ferry to Birkenhead. Connor would eat his last breakfast in this house and then they'd be gone for good. There had to be a better life awaiting them in England.

While Connor ate his Coco Pops, she explained to him that they were going on a holiday.

'Where's Daddy?' he asked. 'Is he coming with us?'

Rosie couldn't prevent tears running down her cheeks, and her throat ached trying to get the words out.

'Just you and me, sweetheart. But we'll have a great time, I promise. We're going to stay with Aunty Claire.'

While Connor finished eating, Rosie made a final tour of the house. She had packed as much as the car would hold, and she checked that she was leaving nothing behind of real importance to her. She ensured that there were no clues lying around that might indicate where they were headed, although she realised that he would soon figure out where they'd gone. She just had to hope that he wouldn't be prepared to come after them. It became a struggle as she battled tears and a deep-seated pain in her chest.

Rosie strapped her son into his car seat and placed the last few items, towels and blankets, beside him. She climbed into the driver's seat with a nervous sigh. She pressed the remote to open the garage door, and slowly it receded to reveal a dismal morning.

'Bye-bye, house,' she said.

'Bye-bye, house,' Connor repeated.

Pressing lightly on the accelerator, the car rolled from the garage, down the short drive and onto the road. She glanced around, fearing that he might be hiding somewhere, but the cul-de-sac was deserted. Breathing easier, she pressed harder on the pedal, and they sped away into the adjoining avenue. They were almost free. They had no need to hurry now, she told herself. There was plenty of time for them to get to the ferry terminal.

A few yards before she reached the junction with the Stewartstown Road, an approaching red Mazda swerved in front of her then braked hard. Rosie screamed. She turned her steering wheel hard to avoid a collision. Her Fiesta mounted the curb and smashed into a garden wall. Connor wailed. The airbag had gone off in the driver's seat and for a few moments Rosie's face was buried within it. She knew who it was without seeing him. Her car door was thrust open, a hand reached inside and grabbed her long dark hair.

Screaming, she was dragged from behind the wheel but became entangled in her seatbelt. Rosie yelled and fought back with flailing arms while her husband leaned over her and fumbled to release the belt. Finally, she was hauled from the car. Her feet struggled to keep her upright. Squealing at her husband, she tried to fight him off with slaps and punches. Then his fist slammed into her face, and she crumpled. He pulled even harder on her hair and, now completely under his control, she could do nothing else but stagger away from the Fiesta.

'Connor!' Rosie wrenched herself free of her husband and ran back to her car.

He caught her arm, twisted it sharply behind her back and again forced her away. The passenger door of the Mazda was pulled open, and Rosie was bundled inside. Blood poured from her nose and was smeared across her mouth as she tried to wipe it away. She looked on helplessly as her hysterical son was pulled from his seat in the Fiesta and dumped in the back of the Mazda. People had emerged from their houses to witness the commotion. Most were too confused by what they were seeing. They were of no help to Rosie. All that could be seen now was a smashed-up Fiesta embedded in a garden wall and a man climbing into a red Mazda.

Without a word, he started the car, reversed onto the road and sped away. Rosie dropped her head into her hands and wept. This was not what she had planned. She'd hoped for freedom, for getting to England and for a fresh start. Her first thought when he had snatched her from the Fiesta was that at worst, he would take them home again. He would demand that she stayed there with him. But he was in such a rage and, to Rosie's horror, he was driving away from their home.

Chapter 16

Ursula fired questions at Sidney on the journey to Shaw's Bridge.

'Do you really think that Martin Shiels was Susan's brother?'

'I don't know,' he said. 'They may not be closely related.'

'But why did Crossley ask you to prove his wife was having an affair if he knew that the whole time, she was merely visiting her brother?'

'Don't know. They may not even be related at all.'

'Do you think that Desmond Crossley murdered Martin Shiels?'

'Don't know.'

'Do you think he's killed Susan too?'

'Don't know.'

'And what should we do next about Terry Quinn and Shane Taggart?'

'Don't know.'

Shaw's Bridge, over the river Lagan in the south of the city, was a popular spot to begin or complete a leisurely walk along the old towpath either towards Belfast city or country-bound towards Lisburn. A car park sat above the old stone bridge now dwarfed by the busy road bridge that had replaced it.

Ursula found a parking space with a clear view of the entrance. She switched off the engine, sighed then glared at her unseeing father. His head was back against the headrest, dark glasses on, his music playing quietly on the stereo.

'Let's see if anything suspicious is going on,' Ursula said, eating crisps, a magazine opened on her lap. She knew full well that Sidney had dozed off. The question looming for Ursula, however, was would anyone show up at all now that Shiels was dead, and it had been all over the news? Who did Shiels usually meet here? Did it involve the exchange of cash, 8K for instance? Were they even in the right place?

Ursula kept an eye on every vehicle coming and going from the car park. There were families with young children enjoying the playground, couples, young and old, having a leisurely walk, and businesspeople making calls, eating sandwiches or having a smoke. She saw no signs of clandestine activity even when she left the van and strolled to the riverbank. Her hopes were raised slightly when she spied two cyclists on the path approaching from opposite directions who then stopped to chat. She, however, looked more suspicious than they did as she lingered within a couple of feet to pick up on the conversation. She decided, however that the subject of torn hamstrings was not relevant to her investigation.

Sidney awoke with a start when she returned to the van and opened her door.

'Enjoy your wee doze?'

'Just resting my eyes,' he replied with a yawn. 'What's been happening?'

'Absolutely nothing. Nobody with a lost look on their face wondering where dear old Martin Shiels has got to.'

'What time is it?'

'It's nearly half one,' she said, sounding bored.

'Do you fancy some chips?' Sidney asked.

'We can pick up some on the way home.'

'You know, I don't think SB stands for Shaw's Bridge,' Sidney said. 'I think it means something else.'

'You have me waiting here for more than two hours and then you tell me that,' Ursula scolded.

Sidney shrugged.

'We needed to check,' he said, 'just in case.'

Chapter 17

Sidney and Ursula were preparing to go out for another session of investigating people suspected of benefit fraud when Sidney noticed a marked police car stopping on the road below their flat. He was impressed by how quickly they had identified him following the incident at the home of Martin Shiels, although Ursula had told him that they would have been recorded on CCTV.

Two uniformed officers emerged from the vehicle.

'Ursula! Police are here!'

'That was quick,' she said, coming into the lounge and pulling on her jacket.

She stepped through the kitchen and opened the main door in preparation for the police officers' arrival. A few moments later and two uniformed constables were standing before her.

'Miss Ursula Valentine?' one of the officers asked her.

'That's me,' Ursula replied, cheerfully.

'Is Mr Sidney Valentine at home also?'

The constable, wearing a flak jacket over his shirtsleeves, had a pleasant face and a jolly demeanour. He looked about thirty; his female companion was perhaps slightly older, but her face lacked a smile, Ursula thought. Murder, of course, was not likely to raise a smile on anyone's face.

'Daddy! The feds are here,' Ursula called, deliberately. She grinned sardonically at the two officers.

'Morning, Constable,' said Sidney when he reached the door, 'what can I do for you?'

'We'd like you and Miss Valentine to come with us, please,' the male officer said. 'We believe you can help us with our inquiries into an incident that occurred last Thursday.'

'Ooh! Sounds interesting,' Ursula teased.

Without protest or further bluster, father and daughter accompanied the officers to the patrol car. Once they had been placed in the rear, the female constable drove them away.

At Musgrave station in central Belfast, Sidney and Ursula were placed in separate interview rooms. Ursula was faced with a detective sergeant named Jones, a burly man with blonde hair and freckles, who began his questioning as if he believed it would be easy to intimidate an attractive young woman. Jones, however, had never met the like of Ursula Valentine before.

Ursula smiled warmly at the nice policeman, just like her father had taught her to do. No need to get nasty in these situations. Besides, DS Jones was quite handsome; she wouldn't kick him out of bed.

'How long had you been having sex with Martin Shiels?'

She raised an eye at the question but couldn't help snorting.

'About two minutes; he didn't last long.'

Jones frowned.

'Only joking,' she said.

'We have you on CCTV entering and leaving his home. Did your father kill Mr Shiels?'

This was so easy for Ursula. DS Jones was wasting his time.

Failing to get answers to his opening questions, Jones changed tack.

'OK.' He sighed. 'In your own words, tell me what you were doing at the house in Deramore Park last Thursday.'

In a room two doors along the corridor the atmosphere was a tad more hostile. When he'd learned of the incident at Shiels' home and that the Valentines were somehow implicated, DCI Harvey had requested to be included in the inquiry since he was acquainted with the private detectives. He'd rushed over from Strandtown station. Sidney wasn't at all bothered by Harvey's presence, except for the shouting and swearing. It was the type of behaviour likely to bring on one of his headaches.

'I thought I told you to keep your nose out of police business, Valentine. That's three bodies in a week. What the hell were you doing at the home of Martin Shiels?'

Sidney was about to respond but Harvey was in full flow.

'We have you and your dippy daughter on CCTV, so don't bother denying it. You're in serious deep shit, Valentine. What did Shiels have to do with the young lads in the Mournes? And don't bullshit me.'

'They're two separate cases, Corporal.'

'Why do I not believe you?'

'You know, Corporal, you really ought to calm yourself down. You're going to have a stroke blowing off like that.'

Harvey loosened his tie at Sidney's mention of a stroke but continued to fume.

'Just tell me what happened, Valentine, or I swear I'll land you in Maghaberry jail for this.'

'We were watching Martin Shiels' house on behalf of a client. He suspected that his wife and Shiels were having an affair.'

'Who is your client?'

'That's confidential.'

'Was that the wife who rammed her Merc at the gates?'

'It was.'

'Name?'

'That's confidential. We adhere to the law on data protection, you know.'

'We'll get her name from the licence plate of the car, so you may as well tell me.'

Sidney made no reply and watched as DCI Harvey seemed to be collecting his thoughts. Sidney recalled the time at school when Harvey had tried to call in debts. Harvey used to lend money to first and second formers so that they could play pitch and toss during break at the smoker's union behind the science block. Most of the kids had no intention of ever repaying the loan and Harvey was reduced to making threats of violence that he was incapable of carrying out. Ross Harvey was and always had been a loudmouth — hot air and little else. He had been bullied as a teenager. As is often said, the bullied grow up to become the bullies themselves.

'So, you're telling me that Martin Shiels' murder has nothing to do with the killings in the Mournes?'

'No idea, Corporal. I was only interested in young Shane Taggart on behalf of Social Security. I was confirming that he was doing the double. I've already sent my report to the DHSS.'

'If only it were that simple, Valentine. Someday I'm going to catch you with your knickers down and you'll regret ever being an awkward sod with me. Now clear off home. I don't want to see your ugly bake near either of these cases again, understand?'

'Loud and clear, Corporal.'

* * *

They had lost an entire day waiting in the police station then having to deal with the detectives' questioning. Sidney was amused by Ursula's response to his inquiry of how she had coped being interviewed.

'Ach, DS Jones was lovely, Daddy. We had a nice wee chat about Martin Shiels and the mess in his jacuzzi after he was shot.'

'Did you tell him anything?'

'Not a thing, but I gave him my phone number, you know, in case he fancies going out some night.'

'What did he say about that?'

'He looked a bit surprised. How did you get on?'

'Same as you, but I didn't give my phone number to the corporal. Don't think he's that kind of guy. I've had a couple of missed calls and a voicemail, though. Desmond Crossley wants to talk.'

'Where is he hiding out?'

'He didn't say, but I'm meeting him later for a drink.'

The police obliged with a lift home to Holywood. It was late afternoon with little time remaining of the day to work on any of their cases. Instead, they enjoyed coffee and biscuits before preparing an evening meal together.

'I got one interesting comment from the corporal when he was ranting at me,' Sidney said as he peeled potatoes at the sink.

'What was that?'

'He was adamant that the murder of Martin Shiels was connected to the killings in the Mournes.'

'Why did he think that?'

'Because we were mixed up in both, I suppose. I told him they were separate cases. As usual, he didn't believe me.'

Ursula looked up from her laptop where she had been checking a recipe for Moroccan lamb. Sidney was filling a pot with water for the potatoes.

'What if they are connected?' she said.

Chapter 18

The Delta Blues Den was a music venue in the heart of Belfast's Cathedral Quarter, an area that only in recent years had sprung to life. Its narrow streets and alleyways were lined with trendy bars, restaurants, new apartment blocks, and crowds most nights of the week.

Sidney, however, was having to share his planned evening with a man who had been elusive in recent days. It had cost Sidney the price of a second ticket for the Delta Blues Den just to meet with Desmond Crossley. He would add the cost to his expenses whenever he gave Crossley the bill for his and Ursula's time. His client had suggested a clandestine rendezvous at Shaw's Bridge. Sidney told him to wise up. This was not a Le Carré novel; he had tickets for a gig, and he wasn't having his evening spoiled.

It was obvious to Sidney when he spied Crossley making his entrance to the dimly lit room that the man was not familiar with this kind of entertainment venue. A business suit and tie were hardly inconspicuous attire amongst denim waistcoats, middle-aged men with ponytails, and mature women in tight jeans and high heels. Crossley, Sidney mused, would be more at home at the Castleward Opera. He smirked at his client's awkward attempts to get served at the thronging bar. When he eventually located Sidney, Crossley held a glass of Coke in his hand and nervously took to the chair that Sidney had been saving for him. Crossley immediately launched into conversation, but Sidney couldn't hear a word.

'Wait,' he said above the din. 'Talk during the break.'

Forty minutes later, the audience applauded when the band finished their first set and took a break. Crossley looked expectantly towards Sidney.

'What do you have for me, Valentine?'

'You're asking me, Mr Crossley? I think you have some explaining to do. My instruction from you was to carry out surveillance on your wife whom you suspected was having an affair with Martin Shiels. You didn't mention that you intended to murder Shiels.'

'Me?' Crossley shouted out then, realising he was seated in a crowded bar, lowered his voice to a whisper. 'I didn't kill him!'

'Are you sure about that?' Sidney was suddenly conscious of sounding like DCI Harvey, asking redundant questions. He simply wanted to gauge Crossley's reaction to being accused of murder.

'Of course, I'm sure.'

'What about your wife? Do you think she killed Shiels?'

'Of course not.'

'She left that house in an awful hurry. We found Shiels dead immediately afterwards.'

Crossley shook his head profusely.

'Not Susan. She isn't capable of killing anyone. And now I'm worried about her. She has disappeared. I don't know where she is, and she isn't answering my calls. What's going on, Valentine?'

Sidney finished his pint and looked expectantly at his empty glass. Crossley eventually took the hint and battled his way to the bar. He returned ten minutes later with a pint of lager for Sidney and another Coke for himself.

'I think we better start at the beginning, Mr Crossley. Am I right in thinking that your wife was not having an affair with Martin Shiels? That she is related to him?'

'Not closely. Martin Shiels was a cousin to Susan's father, making her a second cousin. Not a close enough relation, it seems, to put either one off from sleeping together.'

Crossley loosened his tie. He looked uncomfortable. Beads of sweat surfaced on his upper lip and forehead.

'And Susan uses her maiden name rather than yours?'

'She uses the name Shiels for her business. She is an accountant. For all I know it might be a tax dodge, but she uses my surname for personal matters.'

'What connection did you have with Shiels?'

'None at all. I never met him. I presume that Susan had come across him at a family gathering or perhaps in the course of her work. That's why I asked you to confirm the affair.'

'Why do you think she has disappeared and refuses to answer calls from you?'

'That's what I want you to find out, Valentine. I need you to find her.'

'Missing persons' cases are not my line.'

'You can make an exception, surely? You're already working for me. I can make it worth your while, Valentine, just name your price.'

Sidney examined Crossley's demeanour. He was certainly a man under stress. Either that or he really did not enjoy blues clubs. His face was quite thin, with prominent cheekbones and a wad of wiry grey hair that seemed as though it had been plonked on his head. Sidney reckoned Crossley had punched above his weight to land a woman who looked as stunning as Susan.

'Why did you disappear?' Sidney asked as the band returned to the stage.

Crossley scanned the room conspiratorially before answering.

'I'm frightened that whoever killed Shiels might come after Susan or me. They might even have got to Susan already.'

'Is that likely given that you just told me you have no connection to Martin Shiels?'

'I just want you to find my wife, Valentine, that's all.'

Sidney didn't believe him. There was more to this man than his concern about an extra-marital affair. Surely, he had not required the services of a private detective just to confirm his wife's infidelity. He could have found out for himself.

'You can reach me on my mobile. I won't be at home or the office for a while. Keep me updated, Valentine.'

Crossley stood and attempted to leave. Sidney gripped his arm.

'Before you rush off, Mr Crossley. Have you any ideas on where Susan might be hiding? Any close friends? Do you have another home somewhere?'

Crossley shook his head.

'No other property, and I can't think of any particular friends that Susan would go to for help. Please, just find her, Valentine, before it's too late.'

Crossley eased his way through the tables to the exit as the band began their second set. Sidney ventured to the bar for a decent pint of ale. He hated lager.

Chapter 19

Ursula parked the van in a car park opposite St George's Market. She and her father then walked the short distance into Friendly Street, the drizzling rain doing nothing to help the mood of either one. Ursula was nursing a hangover from an evening spent with old school chums at a bar in Holywood. They didn't meet up often but when it happened, they didn't hold back on the drink. Ursula was beginning to think she was getting too old for it. She was aware of her body clock ticking. On mornings like this such thoughts depressed her.

Sidney merely suffered from the effects of a late night followed by a restless sleep. He had failed to clear his mind of the Crossleys and what they were about. As far as Desmond Crossley was concerned, Sidney had a peculiar sensation of being used. The man had displayed indifference to the death of Martin Shiels. And yet Crossley was the prime suspect for the murder. He had motive. His wife supposedly had been having an affair with the man. Now she had disappeared. Perhaps, Sidney thought, she'd fled in fear that Crossley would kill her too. Or she might already be dead. There was no fixed scale when it came to measuring the jealousy of an aggrieved husband.

A hundred or more people were gathered outside the home of Donna Cassidy. As Sidney and Ursula approached, Terry Quinn's coffin was being carried from the house. A group of four men from the undertakers placed it on a pair of trestles in the middle of the road behind a waiting hearse. Slowly, the immediate family filed out. Quinn's girlfriend Donna was comforted by a middle-aged woman. Several others followed – Sidney presumed they were Quinn's parents and his siblings. Among the mourners, Donna appeared most upset by the proceedings and the woman by her side maintained a firm hold of her arm. A group of six young lads, all wearing green and white Glasgow Celtic football jerseys as a tribute to their late fellow supporter, stepped forward and, assisted by the undertakers, raised the coffin onto their shoulders. Slowly, the cortege moved off.

Sidney scanned the mourners who had joined the procession for any familiar faces. Nothing was so obvious. But Sidney and Ursula had also come in hope of speaking again with Donna if they got the opportunity. Sidney suggested to Ursula that they should walk into town for coffee. It would pass the time while they waited for Donna to return home from the burial. Then hopefully, they could have a chat with her alone.

When the funeral procession reached the junction with Stewart Street, the mourners paused by the Glasgow Celtic mural on the gable wall of a house. The coffin was then placed inside the hearse and the mourners dispersed to go to their vehicles. As a convoy of cars assembled, it gradually moved off towards the city centre en route to Milltown Cemetery.

One man, however, had remained in his car during the funeral procession, and he didn't join the convoy to follow the hearse. He had watched intently from Stewart Street as the procession passed by. When the traffic had dispersed, he simply drove away.

The house on Friendly Street, later that afternoon, was bristling with people enjoying tea, food and beer when Ursula and Sidney returned and approached the front door. A young couple were smoking and sharing a laugh outside. Ursula asked them if she could speak with Donna. The young woman went inside and a few seconds later Donna appeared on the doorstep.

'Hello,' she said cheerfully to Ursula while staring at Sidney. 'Thanks for coming,' she added.

The young lad who had been smoking went back inside the house, allowing Sid and Ursula to speak privately with Donna.

'This is Sidney, my daddy,' said Ursula.

'Sorry for your loss,' Sidney said, shaking Donna's hand.

Ursula was then free to put the question to Donna that she had raised with her father the day before.

'Do you know whether or not Terry had any dealings with a man named Martin Shiels?'

The warmth in Donna's face, the friendliness that Ursula had experienced when they first met, vanished.

'What makes you think that?' Donna asked.

Before Ursula or Sidney could respond, several people emerged from the house and bid goodbye to Donna with hugs and kisses and promises to be in touch. Sidney exchanged a conspiratorial look with Ursula.

'Who are you people?' Donna asked when she was free again. 'Sean told me that you're not Shane's cousins. He reckons that you are cops.'

Sidney's eyes widened at the remark. Ursula handed Donna a business card.

'We're trying to find out who killed Shane and therefore who killed Terry,' said Ursula.

'I never knew what Terry got up to. All I know is that he hung around with Shane, helped him do the windows and whatever else they found to do. I'm sure a lot of it was dodgy but I never thought it would end like this.'

Ursula hugged Donna as she burst into tears.

'Did he know Martin Shiels?' Sidney asked, ploughing on with his questions despite the woman's upset.

'I don't know anybody called Shiels.'

Donna's tears continued and finally Ursula led her back inside her home. They got no further information from the bereaved woman.

Sidney looked pensive as they got back to their van. Ursula said exactly what her father had been thinking.

'Something is not right with that woman. She was quick to distance herself from what her boyfriend got up to, and did you see her face when I mentioned Martin Shiels?'

'She avoided saying anything about him,' said Sidney.

'She's lying through her teeth. I don't think we're finished with Donna Cassidy.'

Chapter 20

Rosie gingerly touched her hand to the swelling below her left eye. The sudden pain caused both eyes to water, although it might also have been down to her persistent crying. She and Connor lay on a single metal-framed bed, a fusty smelling mattress beneath them. They tried to snuggle under a light duvet, but it felt damp and failed to provide much warmth. The room was cold and bare. The once white-painted walls were now dull and flaking. The ceiling was vaulted with the exposed beams of an ancient roof that was holed in several places. There was a single sash window, the grime of which obscured much of the daylight. In addition to the bed, there was one wooden-framed dining chair and an old commode standing in the corner. She had begged him to be allowed some of their belongings in the room but, as far as she remembered, everything had been left behind in the Fiesta.

She thought about the scene of their abduction. Would someone who witnessed it have called the police? Surely, the owner of the house where her car had crashed into the garden wall would have contacted the authorities. Would the police be searching for them? She thought also about her parents. They would be expecting to hear from her, and her sister would be awaiting their arrival at her home in Hampshire.

They hadn't made it far. Rather than confront her in their own home, he'd been waiting for them in the next street. He had told her that he wanted to see if she really was prepared to leave him. But why was he now keeping them as prisoners? Why bring them here, wherever here was? She had no clue. She hadn't taken any notice of where they'd been going. She had been too busy trying to get him to talk some sense. His head must be so messed up right now; he couldn't be thinking straight. She had been his friend since childhood. They'd been married for nearly four years. She knew it was over, of course, but it shouldn't be ending like this. At worst, she had thought he would have brought them home, to talk or even to argue, but not this. She and Connor were his prisoners. And he wasn't prepared to listen or to talk about anything.

Connor drifted in and out of sleep, and Rosie prayed he could remain that way until their ordeal was over. Surely, their captivity could not go on for long. It was better that Connor had no idea what was happening to his family. At four years old, he was far too young to understand.

Rosie slipped quietly from the bed and padded barefoot on the floorboards to the window. She had to kneel just to peer out. There was little to see but a few old farm buildings, white-washed but looking disused. Beyond the old sheds were several beech trees, and then nothing but open fields.

They were hungry and thirsty. Rosie had no idea of the place or of the time. She swept her long black hair behind her, her bruised face was pale, and her slim body couldn't retain much heat beneath the T-shirt and leggings she had worn when she'd fled their house. She didn't know whether to hope for rescue or to pray that he would come to his senses and take them home. In her heart, she realised that things had gone way too far.

In the quiet of the room, she listened for signs of activity downstairs. She was convinced that someone, if not her husband, was staying in the house. She considered how they might escape.

The window was sealed shut from years of neglect and poorly applied paint. She couldn't budge it. The door was locked by a key, and she'd heard a bolt being slid into place when they were first thrown inside. Rosie had already decided that she would smash the window using the chair but would wait until she was certain they were alone in the house. So, she listened intently for the front door closing and perhaps the sound of a car driving away. Even if that were to happen, she and Connor would have to jump from the first floor. The ground beneath seemed to be gravel overgrown by grass, but it would not be an easy landing.

When darkness fell, she listened to the silence for what seemed like hours. She steeled herself to be ready for their escape. But just when she felt brave enough to make the attempt there was a sudden flurry of activity. Car headlights shining through the window briefly illuminated the room. Doors were opened and then slammed shut. Then there came the sound of footsteps on the landing outside their room followed by a bolt releasing. Rosie jumped from the bed ready to be freed. Hope surged through her. The key turned in the lock. She stood in the darkness waiting for him to tell her she could go home. There was a sudden burst of light as the door opened slightly and a brown paper package was pushed along the floor into the room. Before she could react, the door snapped shut and was quickly relocked.

'Wait! Come back. Please, talk to me.'

There was no reply, only the sound of heavy footsteps on the wooden stairs.

She fumbled on the floor until she found the package. She touched the paper and it felt warm. When her eyes had readjusted to the darkness, she could just make out that it was a takeaway meal containing burgers and fries. There were also two bottles of water. She wakened Connor, and the two of them sat on the floor to eat their meal in darkness and despair.

Chapter 21

Ursula hurried to the bar and restaurant on the Upper Newtownards Road in Ballyhack, short for Ballyhackamore, in the heart of east Belfast. Her toes nipped in high heels and her close-fitting dress restricted her walk. She reached the first floor of the building, remodelled from a former bank, and waited for a waitress to approach. Immediately, however, she spotted her date taking a seat in a booth by the window. She unbelted her coat and strolled confidently across the room. DS Jones stood to greet her.

'Hiya,' she said cheerfully.

He smiled and she removed her coat to reveal her little black dress. She was self-conscious, however, that it was cut too low. Too much for a first date, perhaps. Jones couldn't help staring; it made her blush.

'You clean up well,' he said.

He wore a tailored shirt with blue stripes and a pair of navy chinos. His smile seemed genuine, and Ursula settled once his eyes had met hers. At least he wasn't obsessed with staring at her breasts.

The pair exchanged trivial chat about the traffic, the weather, the restaurant, and they chose similar food. Ursula tucked into spicy chicken goujons with fries, while Jones had a crispy chicken burger. Neither one drank alcohol. She expected that it would be a quiet night.

'So, what do you get up to when you're not snooping round crime scenes?' he asked her as they ate.

'I could ask you the same.'

Jones smiled at her wit.

'Tell me about you and Sidney.'

Ursula lifted her glass of sparkling water but didn't drink. Instead, she pouted then smiled, measuring her response to her date who was, after all, a policeman. Somehow, she felt more comfortable talking about Sidney. It was much too early in the getting-to-know-you process to discuss herself.

'Sidney is my daddy, sort of.'

Jones' face lit up at her remark.

'What do you mean, sort of?' he asked, amused yet intrigued.

She was still smiling too. His question had not put her off.

'We both think he is,' she said with a chuckle. 'We've never bothered to have it checked.'

'Sounds interesting.'

Ursula was quite prepared to leave it hanging. She knew little of this man. Three hours after he had interviewed her at Musgrave police station, he had phoned and asked her out. She had been drinking with her friends at the time. They all gave her stick when they overheard the conversation. For all she knew, DS Jones might simply be furthering his inquiries into the murder of Martin Shiels. When she resumed eating, Jones was incredulous.

'Is that it? That's all you're going to say about it?'

She gave a nervous laugh and shrugged coyly. Eventually, she relented and set down her knife and fork.

'Sidney and my mother were together for a while, but they broke up before I was born. My mother is English, and she wanted to stay in England, but Sidney wanted to come back to Belfast. He'd been in the navy for ten years before they met, and he'd been away from home since leaving school. The story goes, according to him, that two years after he came home Laura, my mum, turned up one day and handed me over to him. Apparently, she had a busy career on the stage in London and could no longer look after me. She assured Sidney that he was my father and cleared off back to the Big Smoke. Haven't clapped eyes on her since.'

'Wow! That's some story, Ursula.'

Ursula shrugged indifference at the telling of her early history. But it was more than enough personal information to impart for one date. She attempted to probe him for news of the murder investigation, but Jones cleverly avoided the subject by continuing to ask about her and Sidney.

'How did you get into detective work?'

'You can hardly call it that,' she replied. 'When Daddy left the navy, he worked in security for a while. Then he worked for an insurance company doing claims investigations. That's where he got the idea for his own detective agency.'

'And how about you? What brought you into the business?'

Ursula stared at Jones, wondering when exactly the cop would let up in his line of questioning.

'After Sidney got shot, he told me that he wanted to use his business to fight for justice for ordinary people – the victims of evil, he called them.'

'Wait a minute, Sidney was shot?'

'He was, aye.'

Jones again stared incredulously.

'What the hell happened?'

'Poked his nose into paramilitary business and somebody didn't like it.'

'Did they catch the person who shot him?'

'Didn't have to,' said Ursula, matter-of-factly. 'Somebody else didn't like that Sidney got shot and they had his attacker sorted.'

Ursula took a welcome drink of water, while Jones looked at her in astonishment.

'Jeez, Ursula, that's incredible.'

'Yep,' she said proudly.

'But you haven't told me how you got involved in detective work.'

'Simple. I told my daddy that I would give him a wee hand. Been doing it now for years.'

'Why don't you join the police? Get a proper career.'

'Don't be daft. That would be dead boring.'

She noticed Jones looking rather hurt. She patted his hand.

'I'm sure it's OK, Jonesy, but it's not for me. I enjoy my freedom.'

* * *

Jones lived within walking distance of the restaurant. He invited Ursula back for a coffee and she didn't refuse. Afterwards, she asked to use his bathroom. Inside the well-kept room, she straightened her dress and hair ready for home. She hoped it wouldn't be an awkward departure.

To her surprise, he was waiting in the living room with two shot glasses of schnapps. His inviting smile won her over. Logs were burning in the fireplace.

Later, he took her hand and led her to his bed. Soon they were asleep, but by morning Ursula was to discover that the man possessed a stamina unrivalled by anyone she had met before. They showered together then she bade him an affectionate farewell. She made no plans, however, to see him again.

Her bonus from the evening, apart from the sex, had been his revealing more than a policeman should about an active case. As they lay awake in bed following their third bout of lovemaking, Jones passed on some useful information regarding Martin Shiels. It was Ursula who had precipitated the exchange.

'So, what do you reckon happened to Martin Shiels?' she asked, gliding her hand over his smooth chest.

'He had been shot with his own sawn-off shotgun.'

'Have you uncovered a motive?'

'There were several failed attempts, presumably by the killer, to open the safe in Shiels' study. Access was controlled by his mobile phone which was found lying on the floor under a table.'

Ursula grimaced. She and Sidney had missed that. Shiels' mobile phone, if they could have accessed it, might have provided clues to whoever killed him.

'You think it was just a robbery?' she asked.

'Seems likely, although it still points to the woman you saw running from the house.'

'She didn't look the type who needed to commit a robbery.'

Before Jones nodded off, he supplied Ursula with a possible name for the person referred to as C in Shiels' diary.

Chapter 22

'Good evening, Mrs Crossley,' Sidney chirped. 'We meet at last.'

The woman jumped, spilling coffee from her mug over her expensive cream carpet. She had just switched on the light in her lounge to be greeted by a plainly dressed man sitting comfortably in her sofa.

'Who the hell are you? What are you doing in my house? What do you want?'

The pitch of her voice rose with each question as she backed further away from the intruder. Sidney remained casual, with his arms folded and feeling perfectly at home.

'Get out now or I shall call the police!'

'Somehow, I don't think you will, Mrs Crossley. Do you mind if I call you Susan?'

'Yes, I do.'

'Fair enough. Why don't you make yourself another cup of coffee and we can have a chat. I wouldn't mind one too. Milk, two sugars.'

The woman bolted to her kitchen, but Sidney followed close behind, guessing that she would make a hasty exit rather than coffee. He'd gone alone to the empty house in Cultra for a second look around the Crossley residence, hoping to find something that would help unravel the enigma that the Crossley couple had quickly become. Within a few minutes of his arrival he'd heard a car come to a halt in the backyard. Sidney had then stolen a glimpse of a woman climbing out of a silver Mercedes and decided to wait quietly in the darkened living room until she had either discovered him or had left again without ever knowing that he was there.

Sidney watched as the woman snatched her mobile from the kitchen worktop.

'Who are you going to call, Mrs Crossley? The police would be more interested in you than me.'

She fumed then slammed the phone down again.

'That's better. Now, what about that coffee?'

* * *

Coffee wasn't helping Susan Crossley. Sidney's presence had struck fear in the woman. She had downed a large vodka before she managed to say anything that wasn't an angry protest. Her first rational question faltered with nerves.

'Did you kill Martin?'

Tipping her head back, she emptied her second glass of vodka. Sidney was feeling quite relaxed and was not at all perturbed by the question.

'I'm a private detective, Mrs Crossley, not a hitman. Your husband is my client.'

Despite her highly anxious state, Sidney could see that up close she was exceedingly attractive. She looked, however, to be wearing the same clothes as when he'd last seen her, fleeing the house in Deramore Park. It caused him to wonder where she had been since then. He reckoned, also, that if she kept drinking at her present rate there would be little sensible conversation to be had. He needed to find out what was going on between Susan and her husband, and how they were involved in the murder of Martin Shiels.

Susan Crossley leaned against a sideboard, the one that had the bottles of alcohol sitting upon it. She fixed her eyes upon the man ensconced in her sofa.

This evening, Sidney looked like a man who'd just popped out for a walk with his dog and somehow had mislaid the mutt.

'Did Desmond kill Martin?' she asked.

'That's a better question, although I was hoping you could tell me.'

'How the hell should I know?' Her shrill tone was much harder for Sidney to bear than her good looks.

'Let's start at the beginning, Susan.' He had decided to ignore her wish not to be addressed by her first name. 'But before we go any further, I think you should ease up on the vodka. Please, take a seat and we can discuss everything nice and calmly.'

Susan glared angrily at her visitor.

'How dare you! This is my home you've just broken into. I still have a mind to call the police.'

'Go ahead, Susan love, don't let me stop you. As I've already said, I should think they are quite keen to speak with you too.'

'You're such a smart-arse; no wonder Desmond hired you.'

Ignoring Sidney's remark about drinking, she poured herself another vodka and petulantly dropped into an armchair and crossed her legs. Within her lounge, she couldn't get much further away from Sidney.

'Can you at least tell me your name and show some ID.'

'I'm Sidney Valentine.'

He rose from the sofa and handed her his card. She gave it a cursory glance then tossed it on the coffee table.

'Your husband hired me to confirm for him that you were having an affair.'

'And as soon as you told him about Martin, he arranged to have him killed. I can't imagine Desmond had the balls to do it himself.'

'Is that what you believe happened?'

'What else could it be?' she snapped.

Sidney remained silent for a moment in case Susan Crossley had more to spout. She reminded him of a bolshy Sophia Loren. There was a Latin temperament on display in suburban Belfast.

'The thing is, Susan, I didn't get to tell Desmond anything before Martin Shiels was murdered. I had not even confirmed that you were having an affair with him. I only saw you once. It was the day you visited the house in Deramore Park.'

'That would have been enough to set Desmond off.'

'I saw you arrive and a few minutes later make a hasty exit when you smashed your motor through the gates.'

'So that was you watching me? In a van across the road?'

Sidney nodded.

'I was with my daughter, Ursula. She works with me.'

'Then you must realise that I didn't kill poor Martin. He was dead when I found him. That's why I had to get away.'

'Where have you been staying?'

'That's none of your business.'

'I take it that you aren't with Desmond?'

'No. I haven't seen him since Martin…'

Sidney remained silent. Her admission of finding Shiels did not absolve her from committing the murder. For Sidney, though, the question of a possible motive for Susan to have killed her lover needed addressing.

'Apart from your husband wanting to kill Shiels as an act of jealousy, can you think of any other reason why someone would care to see Shiels dead?'

Susan began to cry. She pulled a tissue from a dispenser on the coffee table, dabbed at her eyes and blew her nose. At first, Sidney regarded her tears as genuine, perhaps the trauma was beginning to hit the woman, though he couldn't help but think that she was avoiding his question. She might simply be a convincing actress.

'Do you know anything of Martin Shiels' business affairs?'

The woman shook her head dismissively then rose from her chair and again made for the vodka. It was a non-committal response. Sidney would require more proof than a brusque denial.

'Why would your husband hire me to confirm that you were having an affair with Shiels? He could have easily found that out for himself just by following you.'

'You tell me, you're the detective.'

'Was he hoping I would discover something else, something more than his wife sleeping with her cousin?'

'Second cousin, if you don't mind.'

She poured another drink and knocked it straight back. Another avoidance ploy, Sidney thought.

'Who would Shiels refer to as C in his diary?'

Susan Crossley glared icily at Sidney. Incredulity or perhaps terror. She was indeed a clever actress.

Chapter 23

A weak morning sun cast a glare over Belfast Lough as Ursula, stifling a yawn, let herself into the flat she shared with her father. All was quiet within; no surprise to her. Sidney was a late riser, but little did she know that he had spent much of the early hours in conversation with an alluring woman who happened to be at the centre of their investigation and a police murder inquiry. The ten-thirty ferry bound for Birkenhead had slipped from its berth and eased seawards by the time Sidney emerged from his room scratching his head and grudgingly acknowledging the presence of his daughter.

'What time did you get home? You weren't here when I got in at half-two,' he said, making for the coffee machine. He was still in his pyjamas or, more accurately, Rolling Stones T-shirt and lounge trousers.

'Morning, good to see you too,' said Ursula sarcastically.

Seated at the breakfast bar, she browsed her phone and sipped tea.

'What were you doing out to that hour? There were no gigs on last night.'

'I met a woman.'

Ursula looked up, flummoxed.

'Good for you, Daddy. Will she be my new mummy?'

'Don't be daft. It doesn't suit you.'

Nothing was said while the coffee machine did its work and produced an espresso for Sidney. He joined Ursula at the breakfast bar and for a moment watched in silence as the Stena ferry sailed by.

'So, who is this mystery woman who kept you out to all hours?' Ursula asked, feigning more interest in her mobile than her father. She was really dying to know all about it.

'Susan Crossley.'

'Do tell,' she said with alacrity.

'I thought I would have another peek at the Crossley residence, to see if I could find anything that would point at a motive for either of the Crossleys to have murdered Shiels. Also, I thought it might be worth checking to see if either one had risked a visit to their home. I'd let myself in through the back door. Next thing, I heard a car stopping in the yard. I sneaked into the living room and waited to see who would appear. Lo and behold, it was the lovely Susan.'

'I think you have a wee fancy of her, Daddy.'

'Well out of my league, sadly. And while we're talking of wee fancy, how did your date with DS Jones go?'

Ursula shrugged indifference.

'Fine. Nothing to write home about.'

'Talking of home, did you make it back here at all last night?'

Ursula cleared her throat. She wasn't going there, not with her father.

'Do you want to hear my news or not?' she said.

'Go ahead.'

Sidney sipped his coffee and listened as Ursula reported what she had learned from DS Jones about the murder of Martin Shiels.

'According to Jones there was eighty-five grand in cash lying in the safe. The police had to break it open. Seems like the motive for killing Shiels was simply robbery. When the robbers didn't get what they came for, they shot Martin with his own short-barrel.'

'Hell of a weapon to have lying around the house.'

'And I found out a possible name for C.'

'Funny that,' said Sidney. 'So did I.'

'You first, Daddy.'

'No, no, I'll pour us some more coffee while you tell me what you found out.'

'I reckon that C stands for Crossley,' said Ursula. 'I didn't tell Jones about us taking Shiels' diary, but he said there were papers in the safe with the Crossley name all over them.'

'Susan Crossley?'

'Yes, but Desmond's was there too. It appears that Shiels and the Crossleys were in some kind of business together. Susan having it off with Shiels is only part of the story.'

Sidney set a mug and a plate in front of Ursula. He had made some toast to go with the coffee.

'Well,' Sidney began, 'that's not the story I got from Susan. She mentioned a guy who worked for Shiels. His name is Ciaran McDermott.'

Chapter 24

Rosie spent her day planning their escape from the cottage. There had been no communication with her husband and his helper, or helpers, except for the delivery of meals. She knew there was more than just her husband involved in their imprisonment, because a man she didn't know had brought their breakfast each morning.

The room was freezing, and she and Connor stayed wrapped in the flimsy duvet. It was a struggle to keep warm. She had asked for some blankets, but none had been delivered. The commode needed emptying but at least the stench was masked by the cold. Today the cottage had been silent between breakfast and lunchtime when a plate of ham sandwiches was shoved into the room along with two mugs of tea. Despite him wearing a woollen mask, she knew it was her husband, but he said nothing. He refused to answer any of her questions. His silence was unnerving. Why couldn't he tell her what was going to happen?

She invented a game just to get Connor to eat something. They had to stare at each other with their mouths closed. If one of them smiled, or even made a sound, they had to take a bite of the sandwich. It took more than thirty minutes for Connor to eat an acceptable portion of food. Rosie tried her best to show her delight, but she couldn't prevent her tears and sobs periodically throughout the day.

'Mummy, can we go home now?' Connor would ask each time Rosie cried.

'It won't be long, pet. Daddy will come and take us home soon.'

Whenever she had settled her son and got him to sleep again, she thought about how to get them out of their prison. She had decided to attack the person who brought their food, no matter who it might be. Whenever they opened the door just enough to slip the food inside, she would try to force the door to open wider, then bring the chair down on their head. Then she would tell Connor to run. If she managed to get free of the room, she would pick up her son and the two of them would get out of the house. When their next meal arrived, she would strike. It didn't matter if it was her husband. She would hit him all the harder.

As darkness enveloped their sparse room, Rosie explained to Connor what she wanted him to do when their dinner was brought to the door.

'When I say go, you run out of the room, get downstairs and out of the front door.'

'Why, Mummy?'

'It's a chasing game, pet. I'll be right behind you, but you mustn't look back. Just run as fast as you can right across the field. Don't worry, I'll soon catch up with you.'

'Can we go home after?'

'Yes, I promise, as soon as we get away from here, we can go home.'

She guessed the time to be around seven o'clock, but there had been no sounds of activity from downstairs. Aside from her intention to escape she was hungry, but no evening meal had been brought to them. A while later, as she rocked Connor gently on the bed, singing songs to pass the time in the darkness, she saw the lights of a car sweep across the window. Then she heard a car door closing, followed by shouted voices across the yard. Next, she heard a car engine starting. Was there more than one car? She guessed there was and that one of them was moving away. A minute later, there were footsteps on the bare boards outside their room.

Rosie nudged Connor awake.

'Connor, remember our game? It's time to get ready,' she whispered. 'But you must be quiet, OK?'

'OK, Mummy.'

Rosie lifted the rickety chair, raised it above her head and stood to the right of the door. Connor stood by her side, but she had to move him behind her to be out of harm's way. She heard him chuckling with excitement. Rosie drew a deep breath and prayed. The bolt was released, and a key slid into the mortice lock. The door opened just enough for a tray to be slid into the room.

Rosie jabbed with her foot and caught the edge of the door. It swung open wide, and she brought the chair downwards into the gap. She knew she'd made contact and a man cried out.

'Ah! What the hell?'

Rosie wasn't finished. She crashed the chair on the man again and heard him slump to the floor. The landing outside remained in darkness. She kicked at the languishing figure and hearing his protestations realised that it was not her husband.

'Right, Connor, run!'

The child didn't hesitate and found his way past the man's stricken body. His tiny feet in trainers padded on the floor and took to the stairs. Rosie still held the chair. She swiped again and struck the man on his head as he attempted to rise. She kicked at his floundering body, dropped the chair then squeezed past him and ran to the stairs.

'Rosie! Come back!'

Frightened by the darkness, Connor hadn't made it out of the house. Rosie found him at the foot of the stairs and gathered him in her arms. The front door was unlocked. She pulled it open and they rushed outside, across the yard, over a rough patch of lawn and into an open field. She heard the calls of the man behind her but kept running.

Rosie had little breath left. Her arms and back ached as she struggled to carry her son. Finally, she had to lower Connor to the ground.

'How about running for a wee while, pet. Just to help Mummy.'

The boy held tightly to her hand as they plodded through damp uneven ground in the darkness. A distant glow in the sky above the nearest town was their only light.

'I'm scared, Mummy. I want to go home.'

'Very soon, Connor. We just have to keep going.'

But then Rosie stopped. They'd reached a hedge of hawthorn and bramble marking the boundary of the field. She couldn't see a way through to the adjacent one. The cottage was out of sight now, but she couldn't be sure whether anyone was still chasing them. The man's calls had ceased by the time they'd made it to the middle of the open field. Tugging Connor along, she had no choice other than to follow the line of the hedgerow. There had to be a gate, a lane or a road and an opportunity to get help. She had no idea where they were or how far it was to the next house. The field sloped downwards and the ground beneath them was rutted and boggy. Rosie's canvas shoes were soaked through. She was cold, hungry, and shaking with fear. They were only a few feet away when she noticed a metal gate and a road beyond it. She helped Connor to climb over, and then she followed. Pausing on the tarmac, she considered the direction to take along the narrow road.

'It won't be long now,' she said to Connor, still gripping his tiny hand. 'You help Mummy by looking for lights in the distance.'

'Why, Mummy?'

'Because that's where we'll be going, and afterwards we can go home.'

'Will Daddy be there?'

She didn't answer. She couldn't answer, not with tears rolling down her face and her heart still pounding. She decided on going to her right, heading downhill. If, in one direction, the road led back to the cottage where they had been held captive, then going downhill might lead away from there. It was tenuous logic.

Fifteen minutes' walking seemed like hours, but she felt some relief in having chosen the right direction. She was certain they were leaving the cottage well behind. A while later, they came to a junction with a wider road. She noticed the sign. Dromara was two miles away. Surely there would be a house or farm along this road, somewhere for her to seek help. They'd only taken a few more steps when she spotted the lights from a house.

'Mummy! I see a light!'

Connor, however, had seen the headlights of an approaching car. Rosie now saw them too. The vehicle was drawing nearer at a rapid pace. She hardly had time to pull Connor to the side of the road when the car suddenly braked. The tyres skidded on loose gravel. Rosie and Connor were caught in the glare of its headlights as it came to a halt only six feet away. Somehow, Rosie knew that this was not rescue.

'Run, Connor!'

The boy squealed in fear. He tried to keep hold of Rosie's hand as they ran from the car. In a few steps his legs buckled, and Rosie had to trail him along.

'Rosie! Stop!' said a loud commanding voice.

They stumbled and fell. Connor screeched in pain as his knees and hands were skinned on the rough surface. Rosie cried out for her son's distress. Agonising pain shot from her wrist and up her arm. The figure of a man stood over them, the car headlights glaring from behind him. She knew who it was, and so did Connor. She sobbed in despair. There would be no escape.

'My hands are bleeding, Daddy!'

Chapter 25

Shane Taggart had lived in the Short Strand area, not far from where he had carried out, among other things, his window cleaning operation. His funeral had taken place the day before Terry Quinn's. Sidney and Ursula had not been able to attend owing to their participation in a question-and-answer session at Musgrave police station.

Ursula parked the van in Arran Street behind the Taggart household. A strong wind swept along the pavement, but Ursula and Sidney were well clad in coats and scarves. Walking to the house, they rehearsed what they would say to whichever relative of Shane Taggart answered the door.

'There's no point in pretending to be Shane's cousin this time,' Ursula quipped.

'Wouldn't go down well, love.'

The modern house was mid-terrace and faced directly onto the main road. Ursula pressed the button of the doorbell then stepped back slightly, not wishing to appear too intimidating. A minute later, the door opened wide.

'Are you Jehovah's Witnesses?' asked an elderly woman with a croaky voice. She was stooped and wore a flowery pinafore and grey fluffy slippers. 'Don't want any of that nonsense round here.'

She had silvery hair, unbrushed, and a waxy complexion. Her weak-coloured eyes were neither friendly nor trusting.

'No, love,' said Ursula. 'We're from the social services. We've been dealing with Shane's case, and we just wanted to pay our respects to the family. I was very sorry to hear what happened to Shane. Are you his mother?'

'I'm his granny.' The woman chuckled. 'You better come in. Founder ye out there the day, so it would.'

She led the way from a tiny entrance hall into a sitting room adorned with ornaments and family mementoes. Despite the modern build and the sixty-inch television mounted on the chimney breast, the room had the air of a granny's parlour with a flowery-patterned wallpaper, brass nick-nacks, and a gas fire burning. It felt cosy and cherished. The woman instructed them both to sit on her Chesterfield sofa, while she dropped into an orthopaedic armchair and resumed her knitting.

'So, is our Shane owed money from the social?'

'No, love,' said Sidney with a sympathetic smile. 'We didn't know Shane terribly well, but we came across him in the course of our work.'

The woman didn't seem impressed and waited for more to be said.

'We heard that he worked with Terry Quinn,' said Ursula. 'Cleaning windows, isn't that right?'

'Aye. Are the pair of you looking for money off me? For I haven't a bean. Don't get my pension till Thursday. Our Shane had me bled dry, just like his mother, God rest her.'

'No. It's not that, Mrs Taggart. We're trying to contact all of Shane's colleagues to see whether their window cleaning business is to continue. To make sure it is properly registered.'

The woman eyed them both suspiciously as she counted stitches. Old, she may be, but she was not going to be easily duped. Sidney changed the subject.

'Do you live alone now, Mrs Taggart?' he asked.

'Aye. Our Shane was all I had once his mother Clodagh and then my husband Bobby popped their clogs. Shane never knew his da, and Clodagh died when he was eleven. Bobby passed away when Shane was fourteen. It was just me and Shane for the last five years. It's lonely now without him.'

'He was a good grandson then?' said Ursula.

'Never gave me any bother, but I know he was no angel. He didn't always keep good company. I suppose that's why he's in his grave now.'

'Do you mean Terry Quinn?' Ursula asked.

'Shane and Terry were a pair of rascals. But they would still be here if they hadn't got mixed up with real bad men.'

'Do you know the names of any of these men?' Sidney asked.

'Ach, love, one week it was one man, the next it was somebody else. A pair of dogsbodies, Shane and Terry. They were an easy touch for the big bosses.'

'It would help us, Mrs Taggart, if you could remember any names that Shane may have mentioned. Even if it was just in passing, it might be important.'

The old woman looked doubtfully at Sidney.

'You people take your work very seriously. You're going to an awful lot of trouble for my Shane. These kinds of men wouldn't be interested in the window cleaning.'

'I know, but it's just so we can complete our enquiries,' said Ursula.

'Hold on a wee minute.'

The woman shuffled to her kitchen without a word. Sidney and Ursula were left looking at each other.

'Would you like a wee cup of tea in your hand?' she called.

'No, you're all right, love,' Sidney answered. 'We can't stay long.'

A minute later, the woman reappeared clutching several letters and a few scraps of paper.

'I was going through our Shane's stuff,' she said, brandishing the papers. 'Most of it's rubbish.'

She pulled one strip of lined paper free and lifted her glasses from the arm of her chair. There was no way, it seemed, that she was handing anything over to Sidney or Ursula.

'Sean Barnes,' she read. 'He only pestered our Shane when he wanted something. I'd no time for somebody like that. I think there is an address here for him.'

Suddenly the papers slipped from her hand and as the woman stooped awkwardly to retrieve them Ursula was quick to help her. It provided an opportunity to steal a closer look at some of the paperwork. She picked out an address before the woman could react.

'Is this it?'

'I think so. Somewhere up in Twinbrook, as far as I know. I've no idea why he spent his time annoying our Shane and him coming from the other side of the town. And he has a family to look after.'

Sidney grinned at Ursula. It seemed obvious now that the old woman was confused by the names of her grandson's friends. They already knew that Sean Barnes lived in Friendly Street in the markets area and not Twinbrook.

'Do you think Sean Barnes would have had anything to do with Shane's death?' Sidney asked.

'I don't know, love. When I said our Shane hung around with bad company, I suppose Sean Barnes would have been a part of it.'

The old woman was now gazing at a photograph she'd uncovered amongst the papers spread on the floor.

'This is Shane and Terry. I think it was taken just last year at one of those rowdy pop concerts. That's my Shane on the right.'

Sidney and Ursula immediately recognised the pair. The youth on the right grinning madly for the camera was the guy who'd slammed a baseball bat onto the bonnet of their van. Terry Quinn, on the left, and looking either drunk or stoned, was the guy whom Ursula had introduced violently to the van door. It was the face of the man they had found dead in the mountain gully.

They refused another offer of tea, expressed their condolences for the loss of her grandson and bid goodbye to the old woman.

'You see, Ursula, that's why I do these things,' Sidney said on the walk back to the van. 'That old dear is alone now because some mean character decided that young Shane didn't deserve to live. We know he was up to no good, but he was loved and cherished by somebody. There won't always be satisfactory justice coming from the law.'

'I know, Daddy.' She hung on his arm. 'That address in Twinbrook might be useful, though.'

'Why's that?'

'It wasn't for Sean Barnes; it was an address for Ciaran McDermott. Isn't that the man who worked for Martin Shiels that Susan Crossley told you about?'

'That's if it's the same McDermott.'

'Might he be our link between the murder of Shiels and the two lads in the Mournes?'

'It would be worth paying him a visit to find out.'

Chapter 26

The Stewartstown Road ran to the southwest of Belfast, leading to the suburb of Derriaghy. The area known as Twinbrook was littered with housing estates, modern private developments and the accompanying infrastructure of schools, shops, and retail parks. Neither Sidney nor Ursula was particularly familiar with the district. During the Troubles it would not have attracted many outsiders. Belfast had existed in distinct cells or ghettos pertaining to one or other religious, political, and cultural persuasion. As the Valentines knew from experience, nowadays the criminals came from anywhere. A political label did not necessarily have a correlation to the scale or nature of criminal activity.

They were pleasantly surprised to discover that the address they had for Ciaran McDermott lead them to a quiet cul-de-sac containing only seven detached and privately owned houses all with mock-Tudor style façades. Number four Pearse Close, also named in Irish as Dún an Phiarsaigh, had a tarmacked driveway to an integral garage and a square patch of lawn in front.

'No car in the drive, looks a bit deserted,' said Ursula.

Sidney got out of the van and approached the front door of the house. He pressed the doorbell several times but got no response. Finally, he knocked on the glass of the door. There was still no answer. He stepped back and looked around the house, gazing up at the first-floor windows and then down the side of the house. All the curtains and blinds were open. Sidney peered through the lounge window. He shook his head as he walked back to the van.

'No sign of life about the place.'

He stood by the van and gazed around the cul-de-sac. Directly opposite, a middle-aged man was tidying the boot of his black Vauxhall Insignia. It displayed the phone number of a taxi firm on a yellow roof sign. Sidney walked halfway across the road then called to the man.

'Do you know the best time to get them in?' he asked, indicating number four.

The man, with thinning silver hair and a ruddy face, could not have looked less interested in Sidney's question. He continued placing shopping bags into the boot of his car. Sidney had now reached the driveway of the man's house.

'I'm looking for Ciaran McDermott?'

The man shrugged a don't-know. Either he genuinely didn't know, or he was being deliberately unhelpful. Suspicion of strangers still ran high in this part of the world.

Sidney returned to the van and climbed inside.

'He wasn't so friendly. No help at all.'

'Do we wait for a while, see if anyone comes home?' said Ursula.

'I wouldn't be so keen on waiting around here. In a street like this, we stick out like a Union Jack on the Falls Road.'

'Then I'll have a go with your man over there,' said Ursula.

She unzipped her fleece. Underneath, she wore a plain white T-shirt. Sidney watched his daughter approach the man, who was now cleaning his windscreen. She posed before him, hand on her hip, running the other one through her hair. The man had at least paused his work to look at her. A minute later, Ursula pranced across the road to the van smiling broadly.

'What's your problem, Daddy?' she said slipping into the driver's seat.

'I don't have your build, love. What did he say?'

'He told me that he hadn't seen Ciaran for a while, ten days maybe. The house has been in darkness at night all this week.'

'Great, another bloody disappearing act. Now what do we do?'

'Home,' said Ursula, starting the van. 'I could do with a wee doze this afternoon. Didn't get much sleep last night.'

'Too much information, pet.'

When Ursula drove from the cul-de-sac and headed for the main road, a car that had been parked in the adjoining avenue slipped from the kerb and followed the van.

Chapter 27

A familiar figure climbed out of his car when Sidney and Ursula arrived home to Kinnegar. Waves crashed over the sea wall; it was high tide and a gale was sweeping inwards from the lough. None of them were keen on pursuing a conversation in the street. Sidney was even less interested in having any conversation at all with DCI Harvey. Resignedly, however, he invited the detective up to the apartment. Ursula began making tea as Harvey said what he had come to say.

'Susan Crossley is wanted for questioning on suspicion of murdering Martin Shiels.'

Sidney gave Harvey a look of indifference.

'Why are you telling me this, Corporal?'

'I told DS Jones that I would have a word with you. I'm guessing that she was your client, Valentine, that's why.'

'Nope.'

'All right, smart-arse, her husband is your client, and I would like to know where he is, too.'

'Can't help you. I haven't seen him since I last spoke to you at Musgrave station.'

Ursula set mugs of tea on the counter for Sidney and Harvey. A smirk spread over her face on hearing her father telling Harvey a white lie. Sidney had met Desmond Crossley at the Delta Blues Den a couple of nights ago.

'Dare I ask if you have seen Susan Crossley?'

'Yes,' said Sidney.

'You have? When?'

'I was answering your question; yes you can ask, no I haven't seen her.'

'Sounds like you're screwed, Corporal, but not in a nice sexual way,' said Ursula with a cheeky grin.

'You pair are hiding something. I could do you for obstructing our inquiries, you know?'

'We've told you what we know,' said Sidney. 'Besides, you told us to keep our noses out of police business.'

The two men glared at each other. Sidney's expressions tended to exaggerate whatever emotion he was portraying. In this instance it said, I've had enough of you, give my head peace.

'I hate you two wise-asses,' Harvey snapped.

'If I'd known you felt that way, I wouldn't have made you any tea,' said Ursula.

'Northern Ireland is a very small place. I can't see the need for private investigators. What the hell is there for you to do all day?'

'Sometimes we get to the truth when the police can't manage it,' said Sidney.

'I'm asking you nicely,' said Harvey with a sigh, 'keep me informed if you hear anything on the whereabouts of the Crossleys. Apart from doing that, stay out of this investigation.'

'Yes, Corporal,' said Ursula, standing to attention.

The DCI glared angrily at her then nodded to Sidney.

'Bye, Corp,' she said to the man's back as he bounded to the door.

When Harvey had gone, Sidney took up his seat by the window, sipping his tea and listening to Radio 4. Ursula joined him, sitting on the matching recliner.

'Don't go too hard on the corporal, love. I know it's a bit of fun at times, but one of these days that man will blow a gasket. He always looks stressed out.'

'I know. I'll wind it down. Harvey thought he was going to get a load of information from us about the Crossleys,' she said. 'He's running around like a headless chicken and it's not even his case.'

'Same as us at the minute,' he said, 'but if we can find this McDermott bloke, I think maybe we'll learn a bit more about the Martin Shiels-Crossley relationship. And now we also have a connection to the deaths of the two lads in the Mournes.'

'And you still believe there's something more to it than Susan Crossley simply having an affair with Shiels? I wonder how that fits in with this guy McDermott and how Taggart and Quinn were involved.'

Ursula, whilst gazing out at the stormy weather, noticed a car parked a few yards down from the entrance to their flat. The driver was seated behind the wheel. It wasn't so strange to see a car parked there, not with the Dirty Duck bar a few yards further along the esplanade. What was unnerving was that she had noticed the same car, a green Volkswagen Golf, directly behind them in the city traffic as they had driven home from Twinbrook.

Chapter 28

DCI Harvey stood amongst the carnage that had once been the luxurious kitchen of the Crossley residence. A forensics officer was collecting samples of blood splattered over the island. There was an incessant crunch as feet negotiated broken glass and crockery on the tiled floor. Stains on the walls indicated where jars of sauce and bottles of wine had been smashed. Several windows were broken including a small pane on the back door. Even to Harvey, the chaos did not appear to be the work of mere vandals who had broken into the house and gone on the rampage. A battle had ensued here. Harvey presumed it had involved at least one of the Crossleys. Someone had fought for their life in this room.

The remainder of the house was relatively unscathed. The master bedroom looked untidy – indicative perhaps of someone having rummaged through drawers and wardrobes – but there was no damage. Or maybe it was a sign of someone's hurried attempt to leave. Harvey had no clue as to whether that would have been Susan or Desmond Crossley.

A badly dented Mercedes stood in the backyard. The bodywork of the boot was crumpled, and it could not be opened. The nearside rear lights were smashed. It was the car they had been searching for in relation to the murder of Martin Shiels at Deramore Park. Susan Crossley was the registered owner. CCTV at Shiels' home had shown a woman hurrying from the house and seconds later ramming the car at the front gates.

An erratic trail of blood led from the back door of the Crossley home across the concrete yard but came to an end close to the Mercedes. Harvey wandered over to the garage. The electrically operated door had been raised but there were no vehicles inside.

At the request of his colleagues at Musgrave station, Harvey had called at the Crossley residence in mid-morning. With Valentine proving unhelpful in divulging the whereabouts of Susan or Desmond, it was considered wise to keep an eye on the property in case either of them had decided to return to their home. Now it was clear that they were too late.

Fingerprints and potential DNA samples were being collected from within the buildings and from the Mercedes. Beyond the forensic evidence, Harvey's only lead in this case, to his chagrin, was Sidney Valentine and his daughter.

One of Harvey's DCs picked his way through the mess of the kitchen floor, stepped outside and met his boss standing by the battered Mercedes.

'I found this in the living room, sir.'

He handed a business card to Harvey. It didn't signify much but Harvey couldn't help smiling at the name.

'SV Solutions. Confirms Valentine's involvement in the case,' said Harvey under his breath.

'Sir?'

'Nothing, just thinking aloud, son. Have we got details of other vehicles belonging to this family? We need to trace them.'

'I'll get on it, sir.'

Chapter 29

Reluctantly, Sidney and Ursula had to refocus on the work for which they were actually paid. It was always exhilarating to be on the trail of justice for heinous murders but gathering information on benefit fraudsters, bogus injury claims and extra-marital affairs was the work that helped them pay their bills.

Four months earlier, a double-decker bus had collided with a car outside the Mater Hospital on the Crumlin Road, a mile to the north of the city centre. The elderly woman driver and her female passenger of a Renault car sustained minor injuries that were treated in Accident and Emergency at the hospital. Of the seventeen passengers on the bus, however, fifteen had submitted insurance claims for injuries, mainly whiplash of the neck and shoulders, and two for lower back pain. The bus driver had been off work suffering from stress since the accident. He had also submitted a claim for damages to his mental health. On behalf of the insurance agents representing the bus company, Sidney and Ursula had been tasked with investigating the validity of the injury claims. At the time of the accident, the bus had just pulled away from a stop and had been travelling at a low speed when it collided with the car. It seemed unlikely that so many of the passengers had sustained genuine injury.

It was a dismal Thursday morning with mist lingering on the slopes of Divis mountain, which formed the backdrop to north Belfast. The sky was in a state of flux. It would either pour down imminently or sunshine would eventually poke through the mass of grey cloud. A weather forecaster's nightmare.

Sidney and Ursula were waiting close to the entrance of Glenbank Park. From an earlier round of the investigation, they had learned that Alex Mehaffey liked to go jogging through the park a couple of mornings during the week. His injury claim, however, stated that, because of the bus accident, he was currently unable to walk long distances and certainly could not run, or play his favourite sport of golf.

Ursula leaned against the bonnet of their van. She could see a figure running in the distance and coming towards her. A fortnight earlier, she had snapped him driving into his local golf club, jumping out of his BMW, gathering his clubs from the boot, and walking briskly to the entrance of the clubhouse. An action shot this morning of Alex Mehaffey mid-stride would strongly support the belief that the bus passenger's disabilities were either false or less serious than he claimed.

Ursula identified him from fifty yards off and stood ready with her camera. When the athletic-looking male in shorts and vest swept through the park gates, she took several pictures. Alex Mehaffey, who had declared on his injury claim form that he needed to wear a neck brace at all times, looked supremely fit and healthy. What Ursula did not notice, when she took the photos, was that captured in her shots was a green Volkswagen parked a hundred yards further down the road.

'Well, I think that's Mr Mehaffey's claim up in smoke,' Sidney said as Ursula got back into the van. 'The next claimant is Betty Downes. She lives in Ballysillan.'

'That's not too far from here.'

Sidney checked his watch.

'Hopefully, around this time, Betty will be collecting her granddaughter from nursery school. Her claim states that she cannot walk without a Zimmer frame. More relevant,' Sidney continued to read from his paperwork, 'is that since the accident she claims that she has been unable to drive.'

Ursula drove the van through the gates of the primary and nursery school at Ballysillan. In addition to staff vehicles, several cars were already parked: parents, grandparents and childminders waiting for nursery finishing time. Sidney had already observed Betty Downes on several occasions. A woman of forty-four, unmarried and living alone, she had claimed that her back and hips had been injured in the minor road collision outside the hospital. When spotted previously the woman had displayed no difficulty in walking unaided or in carrying her granddaughter from inside her home to her car.

Ursula knew the make, colour and registration of Betty's vehicle. The van's position afforded them a view of the main entrance of the nursery building and of the school gates. They could observe cars arriving and they would be able to see people entering the nursery. A few minutes later, they watched as Betty Downes' silver-blue Fiat drove through the gates and swung to a halt not far from their van.

'Do you want me to take this one?' Sidney offered.

Ursula couldn't help laughing. 'After the last time when you forgot to press the wee button on the screen?'

'All right then, you do it smarty pants.'

Ursula got out of the van to wait for Betty Downes' display of invalidity. She took several shots of the woman getting out of her car and strolling to the nursery's entrance. Evidently, the woman could walk unaided, and she could drive a car. A photo of her carrying her granddaughter, maybe swinging her playfully in the air, and another false injury claim would bite the dust. As she waited for Betty to reappear, Ursula's attention suddenly switched to the entrance gates of the school. Parked just outside, half on the road, half on the pavement, was a green Volkswagen.

She turned from studying the car in time to witness Betty Downes emerging from the nursery school building, a young girl skipping along by her side. Betty held the child's hand and swung her arm playfully. It was hardly a definitive sign that the woman was fit and able, but Ursula recorded a short video of the scene. The woman was clearly healthier than her claim had suggested.

Sidney lowered his window and called to his daughter. 'Did you get it?'

Ursula lingered; her gaze focussed once again on the green Volkswagen.

'Yes, but I think somebody is following us.'

When she got back into the van Ursula explained about having noticed the Volkswagen Golf, firstly, on the drive home from Twinbrook a couple of days earlier, then parked outside their flat on the same evening and now waiting by the gates of the nursery school in Ballysillan.

'It's probably one of DCI Harvey's monkeys keeping an eye on us,' said Sidney.

'I'll go and have a word, see what he has to say.'

'No. Not here, Ursula. Don't let him know that we're aware of him. Let's wait till we have a better chance. If he sees you approaching now, he'll just drive off.'

Chapter 30

Next morning Sidney and Ursula had more questions to ask in Friendly Street.

'You spend your whole life never having the need or the inclination to visit this place and now I've been here three times in a week,' said Ursula, pulling up outside the home of Donna Cassidy and next to the residence of the snivelling Sean Barnes.

Donna's attempt at friendliness failed to impress Sidney or Ursula. It seemed like a blatant mask for her unease at having such people calling at her home again. Sidney, nursing a headache, did not remove his dark glasses when he sat down in her living room. Donna's insouciance when she'd greeted them resulted in Ursula scanning the room for something suitable to smash.

'What can I help you with this morning?' Donna asked, with all the sincerity of a bored shop assistant. She reached for her cigarettes on the arm of a chair.

'Well, Donna, I have a question for you,' said Sidney with a smile of irritation.

'Go ahead, but I think I've told you everything I can.'

Ursula lifted a Royal Doulton figurine of a sweet young girl and her basket of flowers from the mantelpiece and examined it. Donna watched her carefully.

'Did you lie to us, Donna?' Sidney asked.

'What do you mean?'

Ursula could see fear sweeping over the woman's face.

'You told us that you didn't know Martin Shiels,' said Sidney.

'I didn't know anything about him. I just heard my Terry mention his name.'

Donna's hand trembled as she drew on her cigarette. There was a sudden smash and she jumped. Ursula had lost her grip on the figurine, and it shattered on the tiled hearth of the fireplace.

'Oops! Sorry,' said Ursula, surveying the debris.

'What the hell?'

'I always find that a bit of damage helps focus the mind,' said Ursula with a conceited smile.

'You two are nuts,' Donna snapped.

Ursula smiled again. 'Ach, Donna, love, do you need a wee hug?'

'You stay away from me. You're a psycho.'

'Tell us the truth, Donna,' said Sidney, 'and we'll leave you in peace.'

'First, tell your mad daughter to leave my stuff alone.'

Ursula, sporting a cheeky grin, perched herself on the arm of the sofa, her arms folded, ready to listen.

'Sean warned me, the first time, that you were going to call,' Donna began. 'He thought I could deal with you better than him. I didn't know you were interested in Martin Shiels. He wasn't dead when I first met you. I just thought you wanted to know about my Terry.'

'We asked if you knew of anyone who Terry might have been involved with,' said Sidney. 'You could have mentioned Shiels then, but you didn't. Then, on the day of

Terry's funeral, we asked you directly about Shiels, but you told us that you didn't know him.'

Donna paced the centre of the room in her pink fluffy slippers. They were a perfect match for the black and pink Playboy onesie.

'OK,' she said with a nervous sigh. 'Lots of people round here knew Shiels, including Terry and Shane.'

'How well did *you* know him?' Ursula asked.

Donna glared with irritation.

'Who are you people? Why are you so concerned about all this? Are you undercover cops? If this is going to get back to the law, I'm not telling you anything more.'

'We're not the police, Donna,' Sidney replied. He'd removed his dark glasses, but his mood was no less serious. This was murder they were discussing. As far as he was concerned nothing could be more serious. His desire was all about winning justice for the victim. At times it sounded much too grand a vocation to explain to someone who had never imagined such a quest.

'Then why are you doing this? What's in it for you?'

'Our everyday work involves the investigation of people doing the double, or attempting to claim benefits by fraud and, occasionally, someone asking us to check on the fidelity of their spouse. Social Security hired us to confirm that Taggart was falsely claiming unemployment benefit. At the same time, Desmond Crossley hired us to find out if his wife was having an affair. That's what we get paid for. But when Shane and Terry were murdered, I wanted to know why two young lads from Belfast that we had been investigating were shot in the Mourne Mountains. Then, while we were keeping tabs on Susan Crossley, Martin Shiels was murdered. Now we've stumbled upon a connection between Taggart and Quinn, and Shiels. It's only natural for us to ask what is going on. So, does the name Ciaran McDermott mean anything to you?'

Ursula became interested in another figurine, a Lladró piece of a ballerina, and she rose from the arm of the sofa. Donna's eyes followed her.

'Not that one, please, it belonged to my granny.'

Ursula smiled gleefully.

'You need to be more honest with us, Donna,' said Sidney. 'Don't you want to see whoever killed Terry brought to justice? He was your boyfriend.'

'I do, but you don't understand what it's like living round here. It's not that simple. Back in the day Martin Shiels was a hero, but that doesn't mean he didn't have enemies. If you keep poking your nose in where it's not wanted, Valentine, you'll be wearing a body bag for your trouble.'

Donna fired a dirty look at Ursula.

'Sounds like you're threatening us, Donna,' said Sidney, 'when all we're trying to do is find out who killed your Terry and his friend Shane. So, tell us about Shiels and his mate Ciaran McDermott.'

Donna's eyes widened.

Ursula let the figurine slip through her hands, then caught it before it hit the floor.

'Right, OK, OK, just tell that mad bitch to leave my stuff alone.'

Donna lit another cigarette and paced nervously in her living room. Ursula had resumed her position on the arm of the sofa. Sidney sat comfortably in readiness to listen to a story, the truth of which he would decide upon later.

'As I've already told you,' Donna began, 'Shiels was well known. He grew up round here. The way he made his money is no real secret. He ran drugs, ciggies, illegal booze and fuel, and he had a hand in people smuggling. He fronted it all with several legit businesses – a nightclub, a pub and a couple of convenience stores. He had dozens working for him, including Terry and Shane. But if you think I'm going to tell you any more, you've another thing coming.' She pointed her finger at Ursula. 'And she needn't think that smashing up my house will get me to tell you.'

She made a face at Ursula, who responded with an indifferent shrug.

'Who do you think killed him?' Sidney asked her.

'He had plenty of enemies.'

'Can you name any of these rivals?'

'The old guard didn't like seeing Shiels become a success. They wanted a piece of the action.'

'You mean the IRA?'

Donna nodded.

'Do you believe that Ciaran McDermott had anything to do with killing Shiels?' he asked.

'No way. He worked for Shiels too.'

'Doesn't mean he wouldn't have motive,' said Ursula.

'No, McDermott was a close friend to Shiels, and he would never bite the hand that feeds.'

'How about Shane and Terry?' Sidney asked. 'Who do you think killed them?'

'That's what makes me think that somebody who was trying to muscle into Shiels' business killed them. There can't be any other reason. Shane and Terry didn't even work full-time for Shiels. They were just a pair of delivery boys.'

'Why not McDermott?' he said. 'Could he have had a reason for killing them?'

'Don't be daft.'

'Do you know where to find him?'

Donna shook her head.

'Nope,' she said. 'Everybody is looking for him.'

'And you don't think the reason that McDermott can't be found is that he's on the run after killing three people?'

'No, definitely not. If you're trying to find out who killed Shane and Terry, you're looking in the wrong place.'

'In that case we need another name.'

'I don't have one.'

Chapter 31

Donna Cassidy yelped in fright.

'You scared the shit out of me! What the hell do you want?'

Irritated, she returned to loading groceries from a shopping trolley into the boot of her car. He had made her jump, but Desmond Crossley didn't really frighten her. He would be hard-pushed to frighten anyone even on a dark night such as this. The man looked bedraggled; his expensive suit was crumpled, and his white shirt held a multitude of dried bloodstains. When he stepped from the shadow into the light, Donna saw his face more clearly. His lower lip was split and swollen and there were several deep and bloodied gouges on his cheeks.

'What happened to you? You look like you've gone ten rounds with Tyson.'

'I had an argument with my darling wife.'

'I hope she came out of it looking better than you do.'

'Susan is quite the athlete. She packs a strong punch. And she's accurate when it comes to throwing things.'

His hand went to his face to illustrate the damage he'd sustained.

'You must have done something to upset the poor woman.'

'She was screwing Martin Shiels.'

'Did you kill him?'

Crossley ignored the question and finally stated why he had come to see Donna.

'I need your help,' he croaked. 'I'm looking for McDermott.'

'Aren't we all, sunshine.'

Unfazed, she closed the boot and wheeled her trolley to the collection point. When she attempted to get into her car, Crossley grabbed her by the arm. She shrugged him off easily.

'Get off me, Dessie. I can't help you.'

'Please, Donna. The police are looking for me. My name is bound to show up among Shiels' files. I've no one else to turn to.'

Donna, still wearing black, in mourning for Terry Quinn, held a steel cold gaze for the nervous Crossley. She stepped closer and could smell his stale sweat. As a young couple walked by with their shopping trolley, she lowered her voice and spoke quietly.

'Listen, Dessie sweetheart, if the cops have got their hands on Shiels' files, then we're all in for it. I worked for him too, remember. And he owed me money. It's all right for you and slutty Susan, you have the funds to make a run for it. I'm stuck here playing the widow.'

She pushed him backwards then opened the car door and climbed inside. Before she had the chance to drive away, Crossley scurried to the passenger door and got in beside her.

'What the hell, Crossley?'

'You're going to help me find McDermott. He must have all the answers.'

Donna shook her head in disgust at the man cowering in the seat beside her.

'Dessie, you're doing my head in. You can come home with me and have a cup of tea. We'll have a word with spineless Sean, see if he knows what's happened to McDermott. But that's all I'm doing for you, understand?'

She drove her Volvo briskly from the shopping centre at Newtownbreda and headed down the Ormeau Road towards Friendly Street. With a cigarette in her hand, she kept an eye on her mobile in its cradle as she drove. She had asked Sean to call her if the police came looking for her. So far, she'd heard nothing from him. The street was quiet when she stopped outside her home.

Crossley followed her into the house like a scolded teenager trailing behind his angry mother. Donna made tea and from her shopping she opened a pack of Jaffa Cakes. Her unwelcome visitor didn't look as though he'd eaten for days. He sat nervously on her sofa devouring the biscuits and watching Donna pacing around the room smoking one cigarette after another and checking her phone for messages.

'Have you spoken to the police?' Crossley asked her.

'Aye, but not about Shiels. They came to tell me that Terry was dead.'

'I'm sorry for your loss.'

'Yeah, well my Terry was an eejit, but he didn't deserve to get shot for it. I reckon, though, whoever killed Terry and Shane also killed Shiels.'

Crossley kept his head down and started eating a fourth Jaffa Cake, but Donna wasn't counting.

'What about McDermott?' he asked. 'What do you think has happened to him?'

'Who knows? He just disappeared. He won't answer his phone and hasn't replied to any of my texts. When did you last see him?'

Crossley sipped his tea, wincing as the hot cup touched his swollen lip.

'Not for months,' Crossley replied. 'He was in the house at Deramore the last time I had business with Shiels. We didn't speak. How about you? When did you last see him?'

'Couple of days before Terry died. He collected the takings from me as usual and said he was going to call at the chippy to see Sean. He told me that he'd just taken possession of eight kilos of good crack, and he wanted Sean to organise the distribution.'

'Do you think that maybe another crowd are trying to take over Shiels' business?'

'If so, they've done a pretty good job,' said Donna. 'Shiels is dead, Terry and Shane are dead, and you're on the run. We're all left wondering where the hell McDermott is. There's going to be trouble for the rest of us if he doesn't show up soon.'

'Maybe he's been killed too?'

'Could be, but the big boss is coming over from Scotland. He'll be wanting to know what's happened.'

Donna returned to her phone, composed a text, and sent it to Sean Barnes.

'So, tell me, what have you done with your lovely wife?'

'I don't want to talk about her,' Crossley replied.

Donna glared suspiciously at her unwelcome guest.

'Fair enough,' she said at last. 'While we're waiting on Sean to show his ugly face what do you know about a guy named Valentine?'

Chapter 32

Desmond Crossley looked unnerved by the sight of Sean Barnes entering the house through the back door. Despite his involvement in the criminal activities of these people, Crossley was unaccustomed to face-to-face contact with many of them. He had assisted in the operations of Martin Shiels' businesses by working the illegal products into the daily machinations of his imports company. It was a business that normally dealt with importing steel and metal components for engineering industries. For Shiels, however, Crossley oversaw the transport of narcotic merchandise from Europe and Africa into Northern Ireland. Occasionally, the imports also stretched to people, cheap labour from eastern Europe and Asia hired as vegetable pickers and farm hands, and young women to staff Shiels' developing interests in the sex industry.

Susan, through her accounting talents, had detailed knowledge of the books for Shiels' empire and for the Crossley imports business. She was a dab hand in the money laundering trade. Bogus clients with fake invoicing for accounting services allowed Susan to process large sums of cash derived from Martin's drug trade. The Crossleys, of course, extracted a healthy remuneration for their work. It had been easy money for the pair and much more lucrative than any of their legitimate pursuits. Now that Shiels was dead, all participants in the business were in danger of arrest, depending on what the police had discovered when they had searched the house in Deramore Park. The knowledge that Susan had also been sleeping with Shiels was an added irritation to Desmond Crossley.

'We need to find McDermott,' said Donna. 'Do you know where he is, Sean?'

The scrawny-looking Sean helped himself to a Jaffa Cake then plonked himself in an armchair as if he were in his own house. He sat with legs outstretched, relaxed to the point of annoyance for Donna and Crossley.

'Who's he?' Sean replied, looking suspiciously at Crossley who returned the favour.

'For goodness' sake, Sean, it's Dessie Crossley. You know that he worked for Shiels.'

Sean nodded at the dishevelled figure, but Crossley did not acknowledge him.

'You need to tell us where McDermott is,' Donna continued. 'He's the only one who might know what the cops have on the rest of us.'

Donna was the only bold character in the room. Both men looked pathetic, Crossley with his fat lip and bloodstained clothes and Sean with the filthy bandage around his sprained wrist.

'I don't know where McDermott is,' said Sean. 'I haven't seen him.'

'Don't lie to me, Sean,' Donna snapped. 'I haven't got time for your shenanigans.'

'I don't know, honest.'

'Give me your phone!'

'Why?'

'I need to see it, Sean, hand it over now.'

'But, Donna, there's nothing on it.'

'Now, Sean, or so help me it'll be more than your wrist that gets busted.'

Sean winced as he pulled his mobile from the pocket of his jeans. He unlocked the display with his fingerprint and handed it to Donna. She quickly navigated to his call list.

'There are lots of calls on here to McDermott. What's he been saying?'

'He's not answering, Donna.'

She continued to scroll through the call list and WhatsApp messages.

'He won't take calls from me,' she said, 'but it looks like he has been talking to you, Sean. Here's one last week when he called you.'

She held out the phone for Sean to see.

'It was just that one, Donna, honest.'

'What did he say?'

'He told me that he had to go away for a while. That's all. Didn't tell me where he was going.'

'Don't lie to me. Tell me where he is.'

'Honest to God, Donna. I don't know.'

Exasperated, Donna sat down and looked at Crossley.

'There you are, Dessie,' she said. 'That's all I can do. We don't know where McDermott is.'

'But what am I supposed to do now?' Crossley asked. He looked from Donna to Sean. Neither one appeared to care.

'You can get the hell out of here for a start,' Donna said, tersely. 'If the cops find you here, then we'll all be in the shit. You're the one they're after for killing Shiels.

Until we find out what the cops have on us, it's every man for himself.'

'Can I go now?' Sean asked, sounding sheepish.

'You hear one word from McDermott you come and tell me, understand?'

'Yes, Donna.' Sean slithered out the way he'd come in.

'Do you believe that guy?' Crossley asked her.

'Not a word. He's a slimy wee git, Sean Barnes, always was.'

'So, what now?'

'Like I said, Dessie love, you need to make yourself scarce. I'll call you if anything happens.'

'Maybe I should ask my private investigator to search for McDermott.'

'I would think Sidney Valentine will only bring you more trouble. Now, clear off, Dessie. I have other things to worry about.'

Chapter 33

Sammy Chambers was a former terrorist made good. How he had accomplished it and just how good was good was open to interpretation. The public display of success of the man was visible high in the Holywood hills above Belfast Lough. Behind enormous security gates with CCTV and stone eagles standing proudly on gateposts, was a dubious illustration of modern architecture in Northern Ireland. Former Deputy Prime Minister John Prescott was in his day nicknamed "two Jags" – a reference to his using two publicly funded Jaguar cars for his political and ministerial duties. Sammy Chambers had six. In Belfast vernacular they were referred to as Jegs. Once asked by a local journalist how he could afford such luxuries when it hadn't been long since his release from prison, Chambers allegedly replied, 'From shrewd investments in the stock market.' Most people knew, though few were able to prove it and even fewer willing to speak of it, that Sammy's wealth came from shrewd investments in racketeering and so-called security provision to local businesses.

Visits to Drumcree Manor were strictly by appointment only. Sidney Valentine, however, wasn't one for protocol. He had no qualms about driving up to the gates and informing one of Sammy's lackeys through the intercom that he wanted a word with the big man. He'd done it twice before and was still alive to tell the tale. It was, however, the first occasion that he'd brought Ursula along with him.

'OMG, Daddy! I never thought a place like this existed in this country.' Ursula gazed at the rolling lawns, the trout lake and the vista of the house, an architect's vision in plate glass and precast concrete finished in a wooden façade, an allegory perhaps for the life of the occupant. Three of the Jegs gleamed in the sun, one in red, one in white and the third in blue. Chambers was Ulster loyalist to the core.

'How the one per cent live,' Sidney replied.

They absorbed the view over the lough before getting out of the van. As they climbed the steps to the front door of the house it swung open, and they were met by a young lady wearing only a silk wrap and high-heeled mules. Sidney was pretty sure that she was not Chambers' daughter.

'Sammy's in the pool,' she said in a sedate voice, Northern Irish grammar school.

She was slim with long blonde hair to her waist and had bright blue eyes. Sidney guessed at twenty, although he was being conservative. She smiled in a sultry manner and then led them through a spacious hallway, her heels clicking on the tiled floor. They went down a short flight of steps and entered what seemed like the spa of a luxury hotel. The elliptical pool had dimmed lighting and a man and woman were chatting quietly together at the deep end. When they saw Sidney and Ursula enter, the woman swam off, clearly nude. Chambers, close to sixty-five, emerged from the water, his wide tummy bulging over a pair of Speedo trunks. He lifted a towel then padded towards his visitors.

'Sidney Valentine! Long time no see!'

'Hiya, Sammy. This is my daughter Ursula. She works with me.'

'How are you doing, sweetheart?'

'I'm fine thanks.'

'Don't tell me you're still chasing after dole fraudsters?' said Sammy, laughing. 'Come and work for me, Sidney. At least you could earn a decent crust.'

'Thanks for the offer, Sammy. I'll keep it in mind.' It wasn't the first time Chambers had extended a job offer and Sidney doubted it would be the last. It was just something to say instead of talking about the weather.

The bald and thick-necked Chambers had no inhibitions about dropping his swimming trunks to the floor in front of a woman he'd only just met.

'Don't mind me, love,' he said chuckling to Ursula. 'Just need to get dried off.'

'It's OK,' said Ursula with a smirk. 'I've seen more in a nappy.'

It was Chambers who flushed. He quickly wrapped the towel around his waist.

'Let's get some coffee,' he said, leading them from the pool into an adjacent lounge set within an impressive conservatory of tinted glass.

'Carol, love,' he called out, 'bring us some coffee, will you?'

'No problem,' a female voice replied from somewhere within the house although neither Sidney nor Ursula could figure out from where it came.

They sank into deep sofas set around a large smoked glass coffee table. Chambers lit a cigarette then offered the box to his visitors. Both refused.

'Right, let's hear it, Sidney. What's going on that you feel the need to speak with me?'

'I take it that you've heard about Martin Shiels?'

'I have, aye. The rumour is that some wee tart blew his head off in a jacuzzi.'

'Near enough,' Sidney replied. 'But it's not certain yet who the killer was.'

'Why are you interested, Sidney? Murder's not your line, is it?'

A young woman Sidney and Ursula presumed was Carol, appeared with a tray of coffee and chocolate cake. In similar attire to the woman who'd greeted them at the front door, she looked about the same age, a young-looking twenty or a mature-looking sixteen. She had slim and tanned legs and her long brown hair fell around her shoulders. Ursula looked on, bemused at the home help Chambers employed. Just how many women were strolling alluringly within this house was anybody's guess.

Carol filled three cups with coffee and set milk and sugar on the table. She left without a word. Ursula watched with a smirk as her father's eyes traced the woman's shapely movements from the room.

The brief interruption had afforded Sidney the opportunity to dodge Chambers' question regarding his interest in matters other than benefit fraud.

'The wife of a client stumbled upon the murder,' said Sidney.

'You mean she is the tart who popped Shiels?'

'Could be. I came to ask you if you know of any disputes going on between groups in the town where maybe Shiels had fallen foul?'

Sidney was asking Chambers, albeit indirectly, if he had harboured an interest in removing Shiels from the Belfast underworld.

Chambers shook his head.

'Not a thing. I certainly wouldn't touch his operation with a barge pole. Besides, tangling with somebody like Shiels is likely to turn political, if you know what I mean. Anyway, he was in bed with Owen McStay from Scotland. Interfere with Shiels and you'd have McStay to answer to. He's a heavyweight.'

'So are you, Sammy,' Sidney retorted. 'I wouldn't think you'd back down from a fight.'

'It's not a fight I need right now. I'm strictly legit these days. I'm sorry I can't help you, mate.'

'No worries,' Sidney replied. 'Thanks for the coffee. It's been good seeing you again, Sammy.'

The woman who'd been swimming with Chambers entered the lounge and sat on the arm of the sofa next to him. She was probably halfway between the age of Carol and Chambers and now wore grey sports leggings and a cropped top that had its work cut out for it. Chambers brushed her leg with the back of his hand.

'Don't forget my offer, Sidney. You're a good man and I can always use one of them. It's hard to find people to trust nowadays.' He smiled at Ursula. 'I could find plenty for you to do round here, Ursula. Give me a call if you fancy it, love.'

'Thanks very much,' Ursula replied, feeling as though she'd just been propositioned by Hugh Heffner.

On the way out to their van, Ursula counted two more young women in the service of Sammy Chambers.

'Jeez, Daddy,' she whispered. 'How does a man that age have the strength to manage all those women?'

'I daresay he doesn't. To Sammy, they're just status symbols like his motors and the eagles on his gateposts.'

'What would you say if I told you I was going to work for him?'

'I would think you needed your head examined.'

She laughed, started the van and drove to the gates.

'Do you reckon he was telling you the truth?' she asked.

'Not a chance. He may not have been involved in killing Shiels but there is no way he'd pass on the opportunity to get hold of his business interests even if it meant a battle with Owen McStay.'

'So, these killings might all be down to a gangster from Scotland. We could be wasting our time chasing round the country looking for McDermott and the Crossleys.'

'If McStay is involved, it certainly complicates matters.'

'How do we find him?' Ursula asked.

'We don't. If McStay is behind this, then we may as well drop the whole thing right now. Much too dangerous and besides, McStay will have covered his tracks.'

'You haven't told me how you and Sammy know each other.'

Sidney was silent for a moment, considering his reply.

'Sammy Chambers killed the man who shot me,' he said flatly.

Chapter 34

Donna had to come alone. Owen McStay insisted on it. Besides, she had no one who she could really trust to accompany her. She had been unable to contact McDermott or, more accurately, he was unwilling to be found.

She was dressed smartly in a black trouser suit and shoes with a low heel. She had freshly washed hair and her swarthy complexion appeared well-tanned. A knee-length overcoat gave protection from a cool morning breeze blowing from the river and funnelling through the streets and across the square at the front of the cathedral. She was a lone figure seated on a bench as teenage boys used the paved area to hone their skills on skateboards.

McStay had travelled from Paisley especially for this meeting. Usually, the Belfast end of his operation would be summoned to Scotland, but the business was falling to pieces since Martin Shiels had met his end. Donna Cassidy, in the absence of Ciaran McDermott and the Crossleys, was his next most senior operative.

A gold Lexus swept to the kerb. At first Donna sat forward on the edge of the bench looking unsure of what to do next. Was this McStay or had this car nothing at all to do with her Scottish contacts? A well-dressed woman in a dark suit and heels emerged from the front passenger seat and immediately opened the rear door. She stood to attention beside it. Then, looking directly at Donna, she nodded once. Donna rose tentatively from the bench and walked towards the car.

The fifty-year-old woman with blond hair pinned up intimated with another single nod that Donna should get in. She climbed into the back seat, the woman resumed her place in front and the car sped off along Donegall Street.

Next to Donna sat Owen McStay, a man who appeared inconsequential, certainly lacking the domineering presence of a gangster, Scottish or otherwise. He was slight, thin-faced and balding. He looked more like an accountant than a rogue although there were those who would say they were one and the same. His clothes were expensive, an Armani suit and tie, and he sported a genuine Rolex on his wrist.

Next to the secretarial-looking woman in front was a youngish male driver, equally well dressed, with a shaven head and designer stubble. Donna was relieved that she also had tried to look presentable.

'Good morning, Donna, great to see you again. Are you keeping well?' McStay's accent was well rounded by education and breeding, although his privileged upbringing had not prevented his chosen career path. His smile looked sincere, but his eyes performed an entirely different audit.

'Hello, Mr McStay. I'm sorry to have to bother you with all this trouble.'

'It's Owen to my friends, Donna. We are friends aren't we, Donna?'

'Yes, of course.'

'Good.'

McStay placed his hand firmly on her thigh, gripping the sides between his thumb and fingers. Donna flinched but tried to smile.

'Now, tell me how we're going to sort out this mess.'

The Lexus was soon free of the city-centre streets and speeding north along the M2.

'I haven't been able to contact McDermott,' she began nervously.

'Why is that important to you?'

Donna hesitated. She was trying desperately to say the right things. She had no idea how much McStay already knew about the killing of Martin Shiels.

'He's the best one to ask about how much the police would have found in Shiels' house that might incriminate us.'

McStay gazed out of the window as they drove into the countryside. Donna's unease grew with every silence.

'What about the Crossleys?' McStay asked.

'I've spoken to Dessie,' Donna answered. 'He doesn't know anything.'

'You think he popped Marty because he was shagging his wife?'

'I don't think he has it in him, unless he paid somebody to do the hit.'

'Any ideas on that score?'

Donna paused again. It would be better to at least offer a suggestion. She removed a card from her bag and handed it to McStay.

'SV Solutions,' he read.

'A guy named Sidney Valentine and his daughter have been sniffing around asking questions about my Terry. I wondered if you have heard of him.'

McStay shook his head slowly yet dismissively.

'What happened to your Terry?'

'He was shot, and his body was found in the Mournes. Apart from that I don't know anything.'

'It's a mess, Donna, an absolute mess. What about Susan Crossley?'

'She's gone, as far as I know, or else she's dead too. She blamed Dessie for killing Shiels. They had a row but since then no one's heard a thing. Could be that Dessie has got rid of her.'

McStay fell silent again. Donna felt her pulse racing. She had no idea if she had said enough to keep herself out of trouble, or if she were about to incur the wrath of Owen McStay. She knew of his reputation. He believed in gender equality. Male or female, either was likely to meet the same gruesome end. It was rumoured that several deep Highland lochs were home to many of the people who had crossed him.

'There's money missing, Donna, a lot of money. Know anything about that, hen?'

She could just about manage to shake her head. No words came. Her mouth went dry. At this point she considered begging for her life.

'It's my money, Donna. I want it back. So, anything you can tell me that will help on that score would be appreciated. Shiels' death is unfortunate, but he's not irreplaceable. There's an opportunity for the person who can sort out this wee mess. Do you know what I mean?'

* * *

Donna stood by the side of the road watching the Lexus drive into the distance. She was still shaking. Somewhere on the way to Larne, they'd pulled over.

McStay's last words still reverberated in her head.

'Three days, Donna. Get it sorted, hen.'

It would take her half a day just to get home, never mind find McDermott, get him back onside and try to recover what money had been lost through Shiels' death.

Donna had severe problems. She knew that the missing funds were the most important thing to McStay. Once the money was recovered, he would deal with the wrongdoers in his own special way. Working for a man like McStay, three days' warning didn't mean that if Donna failed, she would simply be reprimanded or sacked. This wasn't a limited company or a sales job with quotas to meet. Failure meant she would have to flee the country or be the star guest at a funeral. If Donna could not reach McDermott, then McStay would have his people come looking for him and for her.

She stood on the hard shoulder as lorries roared by en route to Larne harbour. Her hands trembled as she rummaged in her bag for her phone. She called Sean Barnes, hoping that he could come and get her. He was not taking calls.

* * *

Owen McStay boarded the ferry in Larne bound for Cairnryan as a foot passenger. Another of his drivers would meet him on the other side. He had ordered his two lackeys to remain in Belfast with the Lexus. Donna Cassidy needed careful watching, but they were also tasked with tracking down Ciaran McDermott and either of the Crossleys. A large sum of money had disappeared from the Belfast business. With Shiels dead, the blame for the missing funds rested either with the Crossleys or with McDermott.

'I dinnae give two flying monkeys who gets in your way,' he told his driver and his secretary. 'Waste them, understand. Just get my money back.'

Tommy McCord raced the Lexus from Larne port back to Belfast. On the journey, Shirley Haig made a phone call to a man she hoped could help them track down the Crossleys. This man would also supply them with the necessary tools to carry out McStay's orders.

Forty minutes later, the car turned off the Grosvenor Road, close to the Royal Victoria Hospital, into a side street, yet another district that had gratefully succumbed to redevelopment. There were several nasty speed bumps that elicited a few swear words from McCord as he negotiated badly parked cars. He found a space fifty yards from the house they were intending to visit. McCord looked for guidance from Haig. It was clear by her lack of movement that she was not going anywhere near the house. It was a job for her driver.

He rang the doorbell of the terraced house and immediately a dog inside barked furiously. A commotion behind the door suggested that the dog's owner was trying to get his mutt out of the way. Eventually, the door opened and the handsome and smartly dressed McCord was faced with an elderly gent in a green cardigan, brown cords and tartan slippers. He peered through thick glasses at his caller.

'Aye, what can I do for you?' he asked.

The voice of the silver-haired man sounded as weak as he looked. It didn't help that the bottom row of his dentures was missing.

'McStay sent me,' McCord replied without ceremony.

The old man stood back and allowed his caller to step inside. He was in no position to dispute McCord's credentials.

The house smelled of food: cabbage or turnip stewing. The dog was still barking behind the kitchen door. McCord was shown into a front room, in bygone days referred to as a parlour.

'Back in a minute,' the old boy said. He carefully opened the kitchen door keeping his dog within.

McCord remained standing, uninterested in the electric guitar and amplifier resting next to the sofa. He did notice the collection of vinyl LPs neatly stacked on shelves to either side of the chimney breast. It was of no consequence to a young man like McCord. Way before his time.

It took much longer than a minute for the man to return. It was closer to five. He held a brown package in one hand and a large envelope in the other. He reached them to McCord.

'All I could do at short notice,' he said. 'It's not like the old days.'

McCord peered inside the padded envelope. He pulled out a Glock pistol and a small polythene bag with a dozen bullets. He raised an eye at the old man.

'Like I said, short notice. The envelope has everything we know about the Crossleys and where you might find them. Don't know anything about McDermott except his address. The word is, though, he's gone to ground since Martin Shiels got shot.'

McCord nodded once but didn't speak and made his way from the house leaving the man to his barking dog.

Haig took the envelope and package when McCord got back into the car. She removed a single sheet and scanned the type.

'Enter this address in the satnav,' she said.

Chapter 35

'I can't tonight. This is my book club night,' said Ursula on her mobile. 'Maybe some other time. Bye.'

Ursula finished the call.

'Who was that?' Sidney asked.

'DS Jones, asking me out again. Bless him.'

Sidney typed with one finger on the keyboard of the laptop they used for business. He was collating their gathering of intelligence on the bus accident injury claim case. Ursula was trying her best to finish *Where the Crawdads Sing* before her book club meeting. She must finish it because likely as not at the meeting Jenna Carswell, the club's self-appointed chairperson, would spoil the ending for anyone who hadn't. It was a novel that Ursula was enjoying for a change. It was a refreshing departure from the period romances the group usually chose for the monthly read. Only ten pages to go. She gazed out of the window. An evening flight was going past, landing lights flashing, wings riding the gale blowing across the lough. She smiled to herself when she noticed the green Volkswagen parked several yards along the street. Returning to her book, she read to the end.

'Do you think he would fancy a cup of tea?' she asked her father.

'Who?'

'The guy in the motor outside. He must be freezing on a night like this.'

'Leave him be. He's not doing any harm. Tell me how to insert a photo into a document.'

'Ach, Daddy, how many times do I have to show you?'

Ursula came to the breakfast bar and examined her father's work. She tutted and giggled at the mess on the screen. Within a few manipulations she had embedded the desired picture in Sidney's report.

'So, where's your problem?'

'Don't you forget, missy, I taught you how to use a spoon.'

'Yeah, yeah, I know.'

She kissed him on the forehead.

'I'm away, I'll see you later.'

Ursula drove along the esplanade towards the railway arch leading to the Belfast-Bangor dual carriageway. As she passed the Volkswagen, she couldn't help glancing at the man slouched behind the wheel. It was difficult to see much in the darkness, but he appeared to be of a similar age to her. He didn't seem to notice her glancing at him. She pondered the possibilities of who he could be. A rookie cop under instruction from the corporal was most likely. An associate of Martin Shiels was more ominous, and she wondered if they might be putting themselves in danger continuing with their murder investigation.

Ten minutes later, Sidney, leaving the lounge lights on in the flat, slipped outside into the stormy night. He wore a navy-blue cagoule with the hood up against the wind and the rain blowing off the sea. One feature of living in Kinnegar, cut off from the town centre of Holywood by the carriageway, was that there was only one way in and out from the enclave of streets. With no through traffic, it was usually a quiet place to live. Sidney at first walked in the opposite direction to the exit, but within a few minutes he'd circled around, passing by his flat and continuing beyond the Dirty Duck. He strolled along the pavement below the esplanade until he was standing at the rear of the green Volkswagen. It was tightly parked between two cars. A quick getaway for the driver would be difficult.

Stepping forward, Sidney knocked on the driver's-side window. He had a partial view of the face within, although mist and rain droplets distorted the image. There was no response to his knock. But the car's engine suddenly revved into life.

The window shattered with the hammer blow. The driver yelled in terror as glass fragments showered over him.

'OK, sunshine, who the hell are you?'

Now Sidney had the face of a terrified man in full view. He was frantically trying to turn the steering wheel to get his car out of the space. Sidney reached in and slipped the keys from the ignition.

'I don't think so, mate.'

Sidney pulled the door open, grabbed the man with both hands and trailed him from the car. The stranger didn't have an opportunity to place his feet firmly on the ground and stumbled before Sidney rammed him hard against the sea wall. In these first moments, Sidney quickly realised he was not dealing with a professional. This guy was neither a cop nor a villain. He was just an ordinary bloke with the terror of the world emblazoned on his face. Sidney kept his forearm pressed into the man's neck.

'So, talk to me, son, or you and I will fall out big time.'

'I'm looking for Ciaran McDermott!'

Chapter 36

When Ursula arrived home from her book club meeting, she was surprised to find Sidney chatting and sharing his whiskey with a man she did not know. He was closer to her age than her father's, with thick fair hair and bright blue eyes. He looked fit and she returned his warm though nervous smile. She could sense, though, that he was not entirely comfortable with his situation. Ursula looked at her father for all the answers.

'Stuart, this is my daughter Ursula.'

The man got to his feet and stepped towards her, reaching out his hand. Ursula accepted it but her look of confusion deepened as she realised who he was.

'Hi there,' said Stuart. 'It's nice to meet you.'

'Is it?' she replied.

'Stuart is the guy who has been following us,' Sidney happily explained. 'In the Volkswagen Golf.'

Had Sidney lost it all together? Inviting a stranger into their home, a man who'd been stalking them for days.

'So, what's going on?' she asked brusquely. She set her bag on the breakfast bar and removed her jacket.

Stuart looked doubtful about resuming his seat, but Sidney intimated that he should sit.

'You need to hear this, pet. Stuart has information about this guy McDermott we've been trying to find.'

'First, I'd like to know why you've been following us?' Ursula asked curtly.

She fired a stern look at Stuart and then at Sidney.

'Never mind that,' said Sidney, handing her a tumbler of whiskey. 'Just listen to this. Go ahead, Stuart. Start again from the beginning.'

Ursula sat, rather cautiously, at the breakfast bar. It was as close as she wanted to get to the stranger. Sidney appeared at ease, however. He even put on a CD to play in the background.

Stuart angled himself on the sofa to face Ursula.

'OK,' he began, nervously, 'from the start?'

Sidney nodded approval.

'I'm Stuart Nichol. I was born in Belfast and grew up in Sydenham, but for the past five years I've been living in Edinburgh. I work in banking. At least I did. I may not have a job to go back to. You see, I've been here in Belfast for the past eight weeks. I wasn't supposed to stay for that length of time. I came home for a week to see my parents. Then I met an old friend. An ex-girlfriend, actually. Her name is Rosie. She's married now, though, to a guy called Ciaran McDermott.

'I've known them since we were teenagers. Rosie was my first girlfriend, but she and McDermott had always been close. They grew up together. McDermott spent a lot of his time living with Rosie and her family. He came from a broken home. His father was murdered in a paramilitary feud and his mother threw him out when she took up with another man. He flitted from one foster family to another until Rosie's parents arranged to care for him. At first, I suppose, I just thought that McDermott was very protective of Rosie, like a big brother, but I soon discovered that he was insanely jealous.

'Rosie lived in Andytown, and I come from east Belfast. Not exactly ideal backgrounds in this country for a boy to get to know a girl. We were still at school when we met on one of those cross-community outward bound courses. You know the type, a residential week in the Mournes, canoeing, hiking and rock climbing. It was great fun, Protestant boys from east Belfast mixing with Catholic girls from the west. Everyone was pairing off; it was only for a bit of craic. It's not like we were supposed to go on seeing each other afterwards. Not at that age and not with us living on opposite sides of the city and of the opposite persuasion. But Rosie and I tried our best to stay in touch. She was lovely. I'd never met anyone like her. She has beautiful dark eyes that sparkle when she smiles, and she does plenty of that. But it was awkward, with school and parents who weren't happy with us seeing each other. So, within a few months of the holiday in the Mournes we lost touch until by chance we bumped into each other on our first day at Queen's.'

Stuart paused and sipped his whiskey. His gaze became vacant for a moment as if he were reliving pleasant memories. Ursula had quickly warmed to this man, and she smiled sympathetically. It nudged Stuart from his thoughts.

'That first day at university was also when I met McDermott for the first time. It was obvious that he and Rosie were close friends, but Rosie made it clear from the start that they weren't involved romantically. McDermott was a cold-looking guy. Not in the least bit friendly, not towards me anyway. He seemed to be suspicious of me from day one. The three of us were on the same English course in our first year at Queen's, and soon Rosie and I were going out. You can imagine that McDermott was not happy about that.'

Sidney opened a fresh bottle of Black Bush and poured generous measures for Stuart, Ursula and himself. It was late into the night, but no one seemed inclined to abandon the conversation. Neither Sidney nor Ursula would have allowed their guest to leave without hearing the full story. Sidney listened to it for a second time, resting his head against the back of the chair. At times he looked as though he'd dozed off, but Ursula knew when he was simply taking it all in. She had remained at the breakfast bar, perched on a stool, leaning on the counter, supporting her head in one hand and enthralled by the tale unfolding.

'We went out for the entire time we were students,' Stuart continued. 'It was during those years I discovered what McDermott was capable of doing. Rosie regarded him as a brother, but I could see that he was obsessed with her. He went everywhere that she went. Whenever Rosie and I were together, McDermott was always close by. He made it clear to me that he didn't like me, and he did not approve of my relationship with Rosie. Of course, he was cunning too. Rosie knew nothing of his jealousy. It wasn't long before he started making threats. One day he pinned me against the wall in the toilets at the students' union. He warned me to stay away from Rosie and told me that she was his girl and would always be his. It was only a matter of time before Rosie would come to realise it.'

'Did you tell Rosie about his threats?' Ursula asked.

'The first few occasions that he warned me off I didn't tell her but then the situation grew more serious.'

'What happened?'

'Rosie and I went away for a week to her parents' holiday bungalow in Donegal. It was supposed to be just the two of us. We didn't get the chance to be alone very often. But McDermott knew the place well. He used to go there with Rosie's family when they were kids. But during that week I got the feeling that somebody was watching us. I didn't tell Rosie, didn't want to freak her out. Then one morning I spotted him hiding behind some rocks that overlooked the bungalow. I called to him, but he took off.

'The next time we went to Donegal, four of our friends joined us. Rosie had invited McDermott too, but he refused to come. I was relieved when she told me that he wasn't coming. I felt more comfortable and safer having the company of real friends. But later in the week, in the middle of the night when Rosie and I were in bed, the mad eejit put a rock through our window. It frightened the life out of us. I knew that it was McDermott and I told Rosie, but she refused to believe it. He ran off and we couldn't find him, so it was hard to prove that it was him. I tried telling her about all the other times he'd made threats, but she said I was exaggerating. She didn't believe that he was like that. He was just being protective of her. She did promise that she would speak to him about it.

'Things settled down for a while but then it all came to a head during a party to celebrate our graduation. McDermott got drunk and started goading me about Rosie. That she would always be his, no matter what. He told me that now that we were finished at Queen's, Rosie would be finished with me. I was drunk too, so I didn't take much notice of him. Then, later that night, he started a fight with my best friend Tom. McDermott soon made himself scarce when he realised that he was outnumbered. We chased him into the street, and Tom, with a few of his other mates, gave him a beating.

'When Rosie appeared, she was so distraught by the sight of him, blood streaming from his mouth and nose, that she blamed me for not trying to stop the fight. That started a huge row between us. We had all been drunk so the next day I thought we could just make up and sort everything out. Instead, Rosie refused to speak to me. Every time I tried to contact her McDermott seemed to get to me first and he persisted with his threats. He did everything to prevent me getting back with Rosie. Eventually, I just gave up trying to contact her.'

Stuart took another sip of whiskey. There was a sound of snoring coming from Sidney. Ursula chuckled.

'Never mind him. I'm still listening,' she said. 'Help yourself to more whiskey.'

'I've had enough. I don't want to start rambling.'

Ursula realised that she already fancied this man. She was enthralled by his story and could happily gaze at him all night. She moved next to him on the sofa, and now that Sidney was asleep, he turned to face her.

'Was that an end to it with Rosie?' she asked, hoping that the man sitting beside her was now free and available.

'Not quite. I had a job lined up in Edinburgh and I had intended to ask Rosie to come with me. I was all set to propose to her. But I never got the chance. As I said, we broke up after McDermott fought with Tom. We didn't see each other again until we were both invited to Jill and Tom's wedding. I didn't even believe that Rosie would show up, not after what happened between Tom and McDermott. But she had also been a close friend to Jill and was asked to be one of her bridesmaids. We sort of got talking again at the wedding and spent the night together at the hotel.

'The next day at breakfast, Tom let the cat out of the bag that I was leaving Belfast to go and work in Scotland. Rosie was upset that I hadn't told her and left the hotel without speaking to me. She wouldn't answer my calls. A few days later, I went to see her, but she wasn't at home. Instead, I was again confronted by McDermott. He refused to tell me where she had gone. I imagine that he got right inside her head. He answered the phone every time I called, and each time I went to her house, he was always there to answer the door. You can imagine the sort of things he said. Rosie didn't love me. Had never loved me. That I should clear off to Scotland and not come back. I never did get to see her.

'Off I went, and I hadn't heard anything from either one for four years. I come home a few times a year to see my family and friends, but I have never met with Rosie.'

'Has there been anyone else in that time?' Ursula again was hoping for a negative answer.

'Nothing serious. I don't think I ever got over Rosie. Two months ago, when I came home, I met up with Jill and Tom. Apparently, Jill had met Rosie at a children's activity day at the Ulster Museum. It turns out that she had eventually married McDermott and she has a son named Connor. Of course, I wanted to hear more about it, so I found out from Jill where Rosie was living, and I went to see her. It took a lot of persuading, and I was surprised when she agreed to come out to lunch with me. But she was nervous that her husband would find out about it. It didn't take me long to realise that I still loved her, Ursula.'

Ursula dabbed at her eyes with a tissue.

'Don't mind me, I'm a sucker for romantic stories.'

Stuart smiled and reached out his hand to hers. She appreciated the gesture by squeezing it gently. Why couldn't she find a man like him?

'Go on, don't stop now,' she said.

'What gave me hope was that I could see that Rosie wasn't happy. She was stuck at home all day. After they were married McDermott had insisted that she didn't work. She had to pack in her job as a teacher. She was supposed to stay at home and take care of Connor and him. Over a two-week period, we had lunch together several times. It felt great, just like it used to be. Then, about three weeks ago, I overcame my fears and doubts. I asked her to leave McDermott and come to Scotland with me.'

'Just like that?'

'No, you see I also had my suspicions about Connor. Without thinking, I suppose, she told me his age and I worked backwards. Connor was born before Rosie and McDermott were married. It seemed to me there was a chance that Rosie got pregnant the last time we were together at Jill and Tom's wedding. I finally plucked up the courage to ask her and she didn't deny it. Of course, I used that to pile more pressure on her to leave her husband. I was so sure she would say yes.'

'And did she?'

'McDermott found out about it first.'

Chapter 37

After such a late night, neither Sidney nor Ursula was enthusiastic about their routine work. Their minds were fixed on matters relating to the story they'd heard the night before. Ursula checked emails on her laptop, a mug of strong coffee beside her. Sidney had donned his dark glasses and had managed only to pad from his bedroom to his recliner. It was unlikely that Ursula would succeed in rousing him from his pyjamas for any part of the day. To her surprise, though, he suddenly interrupted her work.

'I was thinking,' he began, 'and this has been bugging me since the day we saw it.'

'What has?'

'The jacuzzi in Martin Shiels' house. When you found his body, the water was bubbling away, wasn't it?'

'So, what does that matter?'

'Well, the water jets in a jacuzzi usually run for about fifteen minutes then switch off automatically. You have to wait for a few minutes before they can be switched on again. Since it was bubbling away when we got there, it can't have been going for more than fifteen minutes. Someone must have switched it on. Can't have been Shiels; he was already dead.'

'Or he switched it on before he was shot?'

'That would mean he hadn't been dead for long when we found him.'

'So that makes Susan Crossley our killer,' said Ursula rising to the idea. 'She goes into the house as Shiels waits for her at his jacuzzi. She doesn't fancy a bubble bath, so she blasts him with his own shotgun then makes a run for it. Has to be Susan because we went in there straight after she fled the scene.'

There was no response from Sidney for several minutes. He was either mulling things over or merely listening to his music. Ursula continued reading and responding to emails. She noted that she and Sidney now had a fresh case to investigate from the DHSS regarding a potentially fraudulent injury claim.

'Another broken paving stone,' she muttered to herself.

'If Susan did it, why didn't we hear the shot?' Sidney piped up. 'Or maybe someone else was inside the house immediately before Susan Crossley got there,' he added.

'But surely we would have seen them.'

'Not if they were already inside and had killed Shiels before we arrived. We only got there a minute or two before Susan Crossley. Then they hid somewhere in the house while we searched the place, and afterwards when we'd left, they slipped out by the back door.'

'The CCTV would have recorded anyone leaving.'

'Maybe it did, and DS Jones has deliberately failed to mention it to us. Not that he has to. As far as he's concerned, we're still suspects in Shiels' murder.'

There was a stirring on the sofa as their visitor from the night before slowly raised his head. He looked as he was, a man displaced.

'Morning,' said Ursula brightly. 'You look as if you need strong coffee.'

Stuart Nichol yawned then sat up straight. He had a confused look on his face.

'Bathroom is down the hall,' Ursula added.

'Thanks,' he replied, rising cautiously from the sofa.

He wore only boxer shorts and Ursula couldn't help smiling as he padded by. She waited until he'd closed the bathroom door.

'What do we do with him?'

'Give him some breakfast and send him on his way,' said Sidney. 'If he doesn't know how to find this McDermott bloke, then he's not much help to us.'

'I think he really needs us to help him. He's worried about Rosie and her son.'

'That's another complication we can do without.'

Ursula prepared bacon butties for the three of them and they sat together around the breakfast bar. Sidney was his usual quiet self at this time of the day. He didn't do mornings well, particularly after a night of blues and Black Bush. Ursula wondered if there was more to be had from their guest.

'Why were you stalking us?' she asked him.

Stuart looked embarrassed by Ursula's question. His face flushed as he attempted to smile.

'I thought you might know where to find McDermott. You called at his house in Twinbrook. That's where I first saw you. I'd been waiting for Rosie to show up.'

'Has she scarpered as well as McDermott?'

'I'm worried that he's taken Rosie and Connor away somewhere to stop me getting to them.'

Ursula noticed him looking at her. He didn't seem to be a man entirely sure of himself.

'Why are you looking for McDermott?' he asked. 'I mean, I don't know who you are.'

'We're private investigators,' Sidney replied. 'We're trying to find out who killed two young men in the Mournes a couple of weeks ago. The killings now seem to be linked to the murder of a man named Martin Shiels. Ciaran McDermott's name cropped up during our enquiries.'

Stuart's face paled and he began to tidy up the breakfast dishes. Sidney eyed him curiously.

'Do you know anything about this guy Shiels?' Sidney asked.

'I've never heard of him.'

'How about Desmond or Susan Crossley?'

Stuart shook his head.

'Shane Taggart or Terry Quinn?'

'Sorry, never heard of them either.' He quickly retrieved his shoes from beside the sofa and went again to the bathroom.

Sidney looked at Ursula. The pair were thinking the same thoughts. That Stuart had suddenly clammed up. His storytelling of the night before was all they were going to get, it seemed. And it was of little help to them.

After breakfast had been rounded off with coffee, they allowed Stuart to leave, with a promise to contact them if he found anything relating to McDermott's whereabouts.

All afternoon Sidney remained pensive. Ursula knew he was processing this latest story. Give it a while and she would pose a few questions. Besides, both father and daughter were still recovering from a late night and a hangover. There was no possibility of her driving anywhere today. Sidney's proven remedy for over-indulgence was his recliner, a view across the lough, coffee, scones, and the radio turned down low.

Ursula applied a crimson gel to her fingernails, and a Sophie Kinsella novel lay on the seat beside her. She had trouble dismissing the sweet-looking Stuart Nichol from her mind. His determination to win back the woman of his dreams from the nasty-sounding Ciaran McDermott was admirable, and yet an uneasy feeling about the whole episode seemed to hang in the air above her.

'You awake, Daddy?'

Sidney jerked in his chair.

'I am now,' he muttered.

'I was thinking,' she said, inspecting the finish on her nails. 'We've only got one side of the story.'

'What story is that?'

Slowly, he raised himself from his reclined position and lifted his mug of now cold coffee from the table beside him.

'Eugh! That's stinking.'

'Stuart's story about Rosie and Ciaran McDermott,' Ursula continued. 'What if it's the other way around? What if Stuart is the aggressor, and this McDermott bloke has merely been trying to protect his wife from a mad stalker.'

'So, you think Stuart is the male equivalent of a bunny boiler?' Sidney had traipsed to the kitchen for a mug of fresh coffee.

'He could be. Maybe Rosie dumped him years ago and he hasn't got over it. Maybe he's been pestering a happy family. We only have his word for it. Maybe that's why we can't find McDermott; he's gone away with his wife and son to escape an obsessive Stuart Nichol.'

'That's a lot of maybes, Ursula. And how does that help us find our killer?'

'It could be that McDermott has nothing at all to do with any of the murders. His is just a name that has cropped up. The man might have enough on his plate trying to cope with Stuart Nichol pestering his wife.'

Sidney resumed his seat. Outside, the day was wet, the rippling water of the lough an ugly grey brown. The Antrim hills were indistinct and formed a murky interface with the dull sky.

'For the time being, I'm not too concerned about Stuart Nichol.' Sidney sipped at his coffee then continued, 'I'm more niggled about the goings-on in that house when Martin Shiels had his head blown off. Do you think we were set up? Was someone hoping that we would be implicated in the murder?'

'The Crossleys, for instance? After all it was Desmond Crossley who hired us in the first place.'

'Yes, but I don't believe it was merely to prove that his wife was having an affair.'

Chapter 38

'How would you feel about another date with DS Jones?'
Sidney asked his daughter.

'Wouldn't be so bad, I suppose.'

Ursula was driving them down a steep hill into
Holywood. They'd spent the morning taking photographs
of a suspect in another fraudulent benefit claim.

'We need to find out if anyone else has been identified
on the CCTV from Martin Shiels' house. If someone
entered the house before Susan Crossley got there, then it
might well have been the killer. I'm guessing it had to be
either Ciaran McDermott, Desmond Crossley or someone
working for the likes of Sammy Chambers.'

'And if there is no one else caught on camera?' said
Ursula.

'Then we're putting the lovely Susan Crossley in the
frame. And before you say it, don't ask me about motive
because I have no idea. All I have so far is robbery, and
that appears to have been unsuccessful since, according to
DS Jones, Shiels' safe was unopened.'

'Maybe Susan just wanted to end her affair?'

'Bit drastic, Ursula. And if the lovely Susan killed her
lover, how is that connected to Taggart and Quinn?'

Once they were at home in Holywood, Sidney took up
his usual comfy spot on the recliner. The weather was now
much clearer such that familiar objects on the north shore
were easily spotted: the parkland at Hazeldean, the traffic
flowing on the coast road through Whiteabbey, going to
and from Carrickfergus, its Norman castle dipping in the
lough water, and the obelisk of the Knockagh Monument
perched on the overlooking hill. It was too early in the day

to start on the whiskey, so he made do with coffee and a thick slice of boiled cake.

Ursula played footsie by text with DS Jones. She tried her best to get Jones to ask her out again rather than her suggesting it.

'Same place as last time?' she texted when eventually he had extended the invitation.

'See you at eight,' Jones replied.

Ursula had to shout for Sidney to hear her.

'Daddy, it's on for tonight with Jonesy. You need to think up some questions to ask him. I'm away for a shower.'

As Sidney dozed off in his chair, missing the evening rush hour of flights to and from the airport, an expensive-looking car squeezed into a space a few yards down from the Dirty Duck. The two occupants remained inside the vehicle keeping watch on the second-floor apartment that doubled as the head office for SV Solutions.

Ursula did not make the same effort to impress as she had on her previous date with DS Jones. Tonight was a purely mercenary venture. Get as much up-to-date information on the murder of Martin Shiels as she could without ending the night in Jones' flat. Despite having enjoyed the sex, Ursula was not bowled over by the man's personality.

Since their recent encounter with that nice-looking Stuart Nichol, Ursula had a heightened awareness that someone might be following her or Sidney. Unfortunately, this evening she was more concerned about her date with DS Jones. She didn't find the presence of a gold Lexus sitting behind her on the drive from Holywood to Ballyhack in any way perturbing. As she parked the van in a side street, the Lexus drove on by. When she reached the restaurant, the car had doubled back, and its occupants looked on as she entered the building.

This time she was first to arrive, dressed in jeans, leather jacket and flat shoes. She sipped on soda water with lime and smiled warmly when Jones turned up. He looked delighted to see her and kissed her on both cheeks before taking his seat.

'Looking great again, Ursula.'

'Ach thank you, pet. How's things?'

Jones looked as though he'd come directly from work. He wore a dark suit, but it wasn't fresh, his tie was loosened, and the top button of his shirt was open.

'Same old, same old, how about you?'

'Me too.'

Jones grinned, bemused by her reply.

'I can't think of you having routine days,' he said. 'You and Sidney seem to get up to all sorts.'

'And how would you know what I get up to, DS Jones?'

He shrugged his shoulders and responded with a playful grin. Ursula examined his expression and waited for his answer. His grey-green eyes seemed to suggest that something was lurking and would soon come out. Jones was not the type of cop who had much tact. He would make a lousy poker player. From experience Ursula already knew that he wasn't much of an interrogator.

'Well?' she said. 'Are you going to tell me what you're thinking, about Sidney and me?'

They were interrupted by a young waiter ready to take their order for food. They both chose spicy prawns with pasta. If Jones thought that he had dodged her question, he was mistaken. Ursula expressed cold determination in her stare. She reckoned someone had warned Jones about her. The most likely candidate for that role was DCI Harvey.

'C'mon, Jonesy, what's running round that brain of yours?'

'Well, it seems that you and your da are still poking your noses into matters that are not your concern.'

He washed his statement down with a mouthful of lager. Then he waited for Ursula's response.

'Is that all? Ach, Jonesy, I thought you were going to tell me that you've found out where all the bodies are buried.'

'What bodies?'

'Calm down, I'm only yanking your chain. Change of subject. Have you turned up anything new on Martin Shiels?'

He leaned across the table and gazed into her eyes. She held his stare and matched his thin smile. She wondered just how much he knew of what they had been up to regarding the murder investigation. Were they under surveillance?

'You're amazing, Ursula.'

He leaned right over the table and kissed her. She smiled and felt his breath on her mouth. Her eyes sparkled mischievously, but she had no intention of kissing him back.

'So, what about Shiels? Did you find anything else on the CCTV footage from the house?'

Jones sat back in his seat, clearly still in the moment, while Ursula had deliberately sideswiped any notion of romance. He then seemed to realise what was going on.

'That's an interesting question,' he said.

Ursula shrugged.

'Just wondering, that's all.'

He returned her smile of feigned innocence with a disbelieving stare. Ursula folded her arms and waited.

'One unidentified individual,' he replied at last.

'Do you mean besides Sidney, Susan Crossley and me?'

He nodded resignedly.

'A man, presumably, wearing a black hoodie, jeans and gloves, entered the property an hour before Susan Crossley.'

'And what time did he leave?'

'After you and Sidney but before we showed up.'

'He was in the house when we were there? We had no idea.'

Jones raised an eyebrow.

'Honest, Jonesy, we had no idea there was anyone else in the place. It's a hell of a big house. We didn't go into all the rooms. So, you think he's the killer?'

He gave a slight nod of affirmation. Their food arrived and Ursula was conscious of her talking too much about the case. She already had the feeling that Jones now had her sussed. That she was out with him to get information and not much else. But she had one last question to pose.

'Who do you think it was in the house?'

'Had to have been Desmond Crossley or someone employed by him to shoot Martin Shiels.'

From that comment Ursula realised that the police still had no knowledge of Ciaran McDermott, nor were they inclined to link the murder of Martin Shiels with the deaths of Shane Taggart and Terry Quinn, even though it had been DCI Harvey who had initially suggested as much.

Chapter 39

McCord stopped the Lexus on the road outside the Crossley residence in Cultra. He then looked to Haig for guidance. She nodded, and he drove on through the open gates and pulled up by the front door of the house. Haig waited for her driver to get out of the car. It was his job to check out the property. He went to the door and rang the bell. Disgusted, Haig lowered her window.

'They're not going to welcome us with open arms, Tommy love. Give the door a blatter.'

McCord banged on the door with his fist then stepped to the right and peered through the lounge window. Haig got out of the car and made her way to the rear of the house. Immediately, she noticed a strip of police crime scene tape stretched across the back door. She saw the broken pane of glass within it and the other broken windows and then she stood on tiptoes to peer into the kitchen.

'The law has beaten us to it,' she said to McCord who had eventually followed her to the back. 'Kick the door in. I want to see inside.'

To his credit McCord had also noticed the broken pane. He slipped his arm through the hole and soon released the lock on the door.

'My, my, what the hell happened in here?' said Haig, after switching on a light and gazing around the battle-weary kitchen.

McCord crunched over broken glass and for no apparent reason opened the door of the fridge.

'Did the old boy who supplied the shooter say anything about the Crossleys being arrested?'

'Nope,' McCord replied, browsing through cheeses and cooked meats on the middle shelf.

'Forget about the fridge and take a wee look upstairs,' said Haig.

While McCord did as she had ordered, Haig wandered through the ground floor of the house. She noted that little else had been upset to the same extent as the kitchen. In the hall, she pulled a drawer out of a cabinet, its contents spilling across the wooden floor. She paid them scant attention: several unused greetings cards, a box of tissues, a pack of facial wipes but nothing to provide any clues to the present whereabouts of the Crossleys. Continuing her search, she swept the contents of cupboards onto the floor and overturned some furniture in the lounge. Anything necessary to find out what had happened to the occupants. Back in the kitchen, she discovered several letters, mostly bills, lying in a drawer. What she wanted to find, however, was a diary, an address book, notebooks or even a discarded mobile phone but there was nothing of use to her. She went to the bottom of the staircase and called to her companion.

'Anything, Tommy?'

She climbed the stairs and called again.

'Where are you?'

'In here.'

She followed the sound of his voice to the end of the landing and found him sitting on a double bed, his feet up as he browsed through photographs and magazines.

'Are you looking at mucky pictures?' she asked.

He held up one of the photographs. It showed Desmond and Susan Crossley standing on a quayside, an elegant sailing boat behind them.

'And how does that help us, Tommy?'

He shrugged a don't know then jumped from the bed.

'Wardrobes in here are mostly empty,' he said. 'You think maybe they've made a run for it?'

'You think?' she replied sarcastically.

'Maybe they've sailed away on their yacht,' he suggested.

She shook her head in amazement. His usual lack of intellect had suddenly improved a notch. It was certainly not his brains that held her interest in him.

On their way out of the house, Haig called a number on her mobile.

'Hi, Donna love, it's Shirley, Owen's secretary. Any idea where the Crossleys keep their yacht?'

Chapter 40

Sidney had a craving for a good pint and some live music. It was only five minutes' walk from the flat to Holywood town centre and a bar situated close to the town's maypole that for centuries had stood at the junction of High Street and Shore Street. He donned a fleece jacket and a flat cap and soon was seated comfortably at a corner table with a pint of Maggie's Leap IPA in front of him. A quartet of musicians performed on a cramped dais at the opposite corner of the room dishing out their renditions of blues and jazz standards. Sidney knew Bob Farley quite well. The two men, unlike DCI Harvey, remembered each other from schooldays. Bob had always had an excellent voice and he backed it up with a gift for playing the blues guitar.

When he spotted Sidney among the other punters, Bob waved a hello and Sidney saluted by hoisting his glass in the air.

Several pints later, and as Bob played his last number of the evening, Sidney set off for home. He zipped his fleece against the cool breeze and quickened his stride as he walked down Shore Street. The subway, beneath the dual carriageway, was lit quite well, but usually at this hour few people would be making use of it. Halfway through he suddenly became aware of a man to his right and a woman to his left. The strangers fell in with Sidney's step, but he knew this was not a good sign.

'Evening, Mr Valentine,' said the woman. 'A quick word if you don't mind.'

Sidney couldn't help a snigger at the woman's Glaswegian voice. How could someone look so good yet sound like one of the Krankies? The voice didn't fit with her maturity or her stature. The man gripped Sidney's arm and veered him sideways against the subway wall. The punch to his stomach sapped the wind from him, and he bent double coughing. Four pints of ale were in danger of making a second appearance.

'Who the hell are you? I've no cash on me. Card payments only.'

'Not looking for any money, Mr Valentine,' the woman said.

That voice again but Sidney was no longer in a mood for laughing. Instead, he considered which one of the two he would be sick over. As he straightened up, he took in his assailants. The man looked strong and menacing yet very well dressed in a suit, tie, and overcoat as if he'd just come from a funeral. The woman, despite the irritating vocals looked self-assured. Even her smile was unnerving.

'What do you want with me?'

'A wee warning for you,' said Haig. 'Keep your nose out of things that aren't your business.'

'Is that a message from the corporal?'

'No idea who you're talking about. Martin Shiels and Donna Cassidy are none of your business, understand?'

'No idea who *you're* talking about, love,' Sidney replied with a grunt.

'That's right, Valentine. You wouldn't want anything nasty to happen to that wee girl of yours.'

Before Sidney could respond another punch caught him in the gut. He dropped to the ground as the peculiar couple walked away. Finally, to round off his evening, his feed of drink splashed over his sprawling legs.

* * *

It was only at certain times, perhaps when he'd been quite busy about the town, chasing leads, asking questions, and confronting awkward people, that his old wounds gave him some discomfort. There had been two shots, one to his left thigh and the other to the right side of his chest. The surgeon said he'd been lucky. A bullet in the left side of his chest would have put him in his grave.

Sidney, during these times of introspection, wondered what would have happened to Ursula if he had died. She'd already been living with him for seven years when it happened. Maybe her mother would have come back for her, taken her to England but then again maybe not. He had not heard from her since the day she'd brought Ursula to Belfast. Since then, she had never once called him to check on how Ursula was doing at school, or even at the time of the shooting. There were no Christmas or birthday presents, not even a card. Now, he and Ursula were completely devoted to each other, although he would prefer to see her settled, married with kids and a nice house. She couldn't keep riding the range with him for ever and a day.

He nursed the glass of whiskey in his lap, his feet resting on the low window ledge. Lights dazzled in the sprinkling of raindrops on the window. A small container vessel motored towards the docks.

The murder of Martin Shiels was less of a concern to Sidney than the deaths of Taggart and Quinn. Shiels had probably deserved it, and besides a violent death was always going to catch up with a man who dealt in the misery of others for his financial gain. But two young lads, however wayward, were still young lads relatively innocent of life, and yet apparently killed for cheap reasons. He and Ursula would strive for justice. That was his motivation. He winced from the sudden burst of burning pain in his stomach. That Scottish bloke didn't know his own strength. He was mulling over the reason for him being attacked on his way home, when he heard his daughter come in.

'Well, Daddy, just as we thought.'

Ursula had a habit of starting in the middle of a conversation as she came through the door. You were expected to know exactly what she was talking about. She tossed her bag on the sofa and removed her jacket.

'Jonesy told me that there was someone else inside Shiels' house, and he was still there when we went in.'

'Does he know who it was?'

'Not a clue. He's banking the entire case on it being Desmond Crossley, the jealous husband; crime of passion and all that nonsense.'

She came to the window and planted a kiss on Sidney's forehead.

'You're home early, love,' he said wearily.

He winced from the pain in his gut when he tried to reposition himself on his chair, but he didn't want Ursula to notice. He had decided not to share the news of his encounter in the subway with her, because she worried more about him than she ever did about herself.

'I think Jones realised that I wasn't there for a romantic evening. He was disappointed when I told him I needed to get home early.'

Ursula went to the fridge, kicking off her shoes as she opened the door. A bottle of sauvignon blanc was already chilled on the shelf. She poured a large glass then joined her father by the window. She thought it was a bleak evening for him to be gazing at the lough, but at home Sidney was a creature of habit. If there was nothing interesting to watch on TV, then blues, whiskey and gazing outside were his relaxants. She thought he looked very tired, though.

'Where do we go from here?' she asked.

'If there was an intruder in Shiels' house, then it had to be one of three people.'

'Desmond Crossley, Ciaran McDermott and who else?' Ursula asked with a sigh. They had already considered the possibilities albeit before they had it confirmed that another person had been inside the house.

'Somebody who works for Owen McStay.'

She laughed then sipped her wine.

'The godfather from Glasgow?' she said. 'What about Donna? We don't know for sure that the killer was a man. Do you think there is any chance that Sammy Chambers got an early start on the whole thing and is intent on wiping out the entire bunch?'

'I can imagine Chambers bumping off Shiels, but I don't think he would bother with dogsbodies like Taggart and Quinn.'

'And Ciaran McDermott?'

'He remains a mystery, considering what young Nichol told us about him. But he might be dead too.'

'Then who do we seek out next?' Ursula asked.

'I've been trying to call Desmond Crossley again, but he's still not answering his phone.'

'How about Susan?'

'I imagine she's long gone.'

'Or dead,' said Ursula.

'Then DS Jones could be right. It is a crime of passion and Desmond Crossley has seen off his wife and her lover.'

'Dare I say it again, but that does not explain Taggart and Quinn.'

Chapter 41

Sidney and Ursula's voluntary investigation into the murders of Shane Taggart and Terry Quinn had stalled completely. Over breakfast at a coffee shop in High Street they again pondered the details in Martin Shiels' diary.

'Does it even matter?' Ursula posed the question as Sidney flicked from one page to the next. 'The initial C could refer to either of the Crossleys, to Ciaran McDermott or even Donna Cassidy.'

Sidney didn't respond. Ursula continued.

'If SB didn't stand for Shaw's Bridge, then it probably refers to Sean Barnes or even someone or some place we haven't identified.'

Sidney looked at his daughter as if a light had just come on in his head.

'C for Cassidy.'

'Yes, Daddy, that's right, C is for Cassidy,' Ursula teased. 'You sound like Sesame Street.'

'That woman is at the centre of it all,' Sidney continued, ignoring his daughter's jibe. 'Terry Quinn was her boyfriend; she worked for Shiels and when we asked her about McDermott, she defended him. She's been fobbing us off with vagaries and misdirection.'

It had just occurred to Sidney that McStay's lackeys could only have known about him through Donna. She had sent the two Glaswegians to scare him off. He had still not told Ursula of his encounter in the subway.

'That woman,' he said, sounding bitter, 'is up to something.'

'Surely, you don't believe that she's behind the murder of her own boyfriend?'

'Why not?' Sidney replied. 'We know nothing about their relationship or how they fitted into Shiels' operation.'

'Then she must be trying to protect McDermott. You think she knows where to find him?'

'She may be simply protecting herself and her position within McStay's organisation.'

'Now you're hurting my head.'

* * *

It was a clear yet blustery morning, and after breakfast Sidney ventured out for a stroll along the coastal path. If he felt up to it, he could manage to walk all the way to Bangor, where he would refresh himself with a coffee and pastry before catching the train back to Holywood. He would round off his afternoon with a pint of Guinness at the Dirty Duck where Ursula would join him later for tea.

Alone in the flat, Ursula caught up with doing laundry then continued reading the latest novel from her book club. Jenna Carswell, club chairperson, was now, it seemed, intent on wading through the Man Booker shortlist. Ursula couldn't see herself getting to the end of this particular tome. Her first interruption came from DS Jones who telephoned in the hope of securing another date. Despite her quashing any romantic notions the last time they'd met, it appeared that he was still quite smitten by her quirky charm.

'Can't make it tonight, Jonesy love. I have archery club this evening.'

'How about Saturday?'

'Girls' night out, sorry.'

'Next Tuesday?'

'Aikido on Tuesdays.'

'You're a hard girl to pin down, Ursula. When can you fit me in?'

'I'll give you a call at the end of next week, how's that?'

'I suppose it will have to do.'

She finished her conversation with Jones just as the landline telephone rang. The voice was not so friendly.

'Is he there?'

Ursula pretended not to recognise his gruff tone.

'Who's calling, please?'

'You know damn well who I am,' Harvey snapped. 'Is your da at home?'

'Please hold on and I will check. Your call is important to us.'

'Cut the crap, love. Is he there or not?'

'Not at the minute. Is there anything I can help you with, Corporal?'

'Don't call me corporal, missy. I can just about take it from your old man, but I won't put up with it from you. Tell him to phone me when he gets in.' The line went dead as Harvey cut the call.

Ursula shrugged indifference and returned to her reading. Then she thought it might be wise to send a text to her father and deliver Harvey's request.

Ten minutes later, her mobile rang. It was Sidney.

'What's up?' she asked.

'I've just been speaking to the corporal. They've found Desmond Crossley.'

Chapter 42

'Security staff at Bangor Marina found him on his boat. He's been shot dead,' Sidney explained to Ursula. 'I'm coming past Pickie Pool now, so I'll be there in five minutes if you want to meet me.'

'OK, I'm on my way.'

Ursula drove the van to Bangor and found Sidney by the entrance to the marina. A police cordon had been set up around the boatyard and adjoining car park. Ursula spied the vessel in question, a thirty-five-foot yacht out of the water for winter and perched on a trailer within a row of five other craft. A forensics team were at work on board and in the surrounding area within the boatyard. DCI Harvey was talking to her father as she approached on foot. The acerbic detective did not acknowledge her arrival but continued to rant at Sidney.

'Crossley was your client, Valentine. Don't try to tell me you know nothing about this.'

Sidney maintained a casual demeanour, standing with his hands in his anorak pockets and smiling thinly.

'What is it that you think I can tell you, Corporal?'

'You can tell me where to find the victim's wife for a start.'

'Your guess is as good as mine. But I reckon she's skipped the country, either before or just after this murder took place, or maybe she's dead too.'

'You think that she did it?'

'Not if she's already dead,' Sidney answered with a thin smile and his eyes wide.

Harvey glared at Sidney and Ursula. He scratched his head in frustration then contemplated his feet.

'You're doing my head in, the pair of you. There's more to this than you're sharing with me. If I had the resources, I'd have a pair of uniforms following your every move. I don't know why I bothered calling you about this. Get out of here before I lose the bap.'

* * *

Sidney and Ursula strolled along the quayside above the marina and bought coffees from a mobile vendor beside the kiddie train at Pickie Pool. They sat on a bench and watched several swan boats paddling around on the water, young children laughing in delight as they narrowly avoided a collision. Ursula waited for Sidney to open the discussion, but he continued to gaze vacantly at the people enjoying an afternoon of harmless fun on the boating pool.

'That scuppers the police investigation of who shot Martin Shiels,' she said. 'They'd pinned their hopes on Desmond Crossley.'

Sidney took a cautious sip of his piping hot coffee. It would be a moment or two before he replied. Ursula did the same. She was in no hurry, her day for relaxing was now stamped with another murder.

'Do you think that maybe we've been looking at this the wrong way?' Sidney asked her.

'How do you mean?' It seemed to Ursula that her father was now posing this same question on a daily basis.

'We've assumed that these killings are either the results of the Crossleys in a marital dispute, or that all the victims have been caught up in the underhand activities of Martin Shiels. But what if we're wrong. What if something entirely separate is going on?'

'Could be something with this McDermott bloke. Or there's your mate Sammy Chambers. Or even Owen McStay.'

'That's what I'm thinking but until we track down McDermott, we have nothing. We'll not get anything more out of Chambers, and McStay is a no-go area.'

'Or,' Ursula ventured, 'as we said this morning, Donna Cassidy has more to tell, and at least we can get to her.'

'Another thing,' said Sidney.

'What's that?'

'Desmond Crossley hadn't paid us a penny for our services and now he's dead.'

Chapter 43

The following day Sidney was standing on the esplanade not far from his flat watching a gigantic cruise ship approach the harbour when his mobile rang.

'This is Donna Cassidy. Have you found McDermott yet?'

'No. I haven't, Donna. I was still hoping that you were going to help on that score.'

'I've no idea where he is, but I need to find him urgently.'

'Why is that?'

'There are other people looking for him, and if they get to him first, he is a dead man. If I don't find McDermott soon, I'll be dead too. You have to help me, Valentine.'

Sidney invited Donna to his flat and told her to meet him there in an hour.

* * *

Donna looked uneasy when she saw that Ursula would be joining them. Ursula, sensing the woman's discomfort, knew how to act her jolly self just to annoy.

'How's Donna? Got yourself any new ornaments lately?'

Donna more winced than smiled, then fixed her gaze on Sidney. Over coffee and pastries for father and daughter only, Sidney headed the discussion. Donna, looking miserable, sat with a cup of tea untouched.

'If you want our help, you have to be completely honest with us, Donna,' he said, gravely.

'I've told you everything I know, honest to God.'

'Only because we dragged it out of you,' said Ursula.

Donna was about to argue but seemed to think the better of it.

'I'm sorry,' she said. 'What else do you want to know?'

'Everything, from the top down,' said Sidney. 'Who do you really work for?'

'I'll get a bullet in the head for telling you that.'

'Seems like there's a bullet with your name on it already, Donna,' said Ursula.

'There'll be one for you and your daddy if I tell you, love.'

'Don't let that stop you... love,' Ursula replied, sarcastically.

'Owen McStay?' Donna blurted. 'You heard of him?'

Sidney and Ursula nodded.

'He runs drugs and people into Scotland, the north of England and Ireland. He has links to Albania, Montenegro and Croatia, and rumour has it to a Mexican cartel.'

'What's his problem?' Sidney asked. He now had it confirmed that his attackers in the subway had been McStay's people.

'Martin Shiels ran McStay's operation in Belfast,' Donna continued. 'Obviously, the business has been interrupted since Shiels got shot. McStay came over here wanting to know what's going on. He told me that a lot of his money has gone missing. I had to tell him about McDermott disappearing and that nobody's heard from him since Shiels' murder. I've been ordered to find

McDermott so that McStay can have a word with him, if you know what I mean. He's given me three days to find him or else I'm tatey bread.'

'You should have told us sooner that you work for these people,' said Ursula.

Donna glared angrily at her.

'I wasn't telling you when I knew nothing about you. Couldn't trust you, could I?'

'And now you do?' Sidney asked her.

'I have no choice.'

'Do you believe that McDermott killed Shiels?' Ursula asked.

'No. It has to be Crossley,' Donna replied.

'Desmond Crossley is dead,' Sidney put in.

'What? I didn't hear about that. What happened?'

'Somebody shot him on his boat in Bangor. He must have been hiding there since Shiels was murdered.'

'Then it was the wife, Susan.'

Sidney winced at the remark.

'There was someone else,' he said, 'besides Susan Crossley at the house on the day Shiels was killed. Whoever it was, I believe, was the killer. There's a chance that person was McDermott. It's time to stop protecting him. You need to give him up, Donna.'

'Honestly! I don't know where he is or how to find him.' Donna had to wipe tears from her eyes with a tissue. 'I need to get out of here.' She peered outside onto the esplanade. 'They could be watching me.'

'Hold on, Donna. If you want our help, you must tell us the rest,' said Sidney.

Ursula placed her hand on Donna's arm, but the woman quickly pulled away.

'I've told you everything,' she sobbed.

'What do you know about a guy called Stuart Nichol?' Ursula asked.

Donna shook her head and wiped her nose. 'Nothing, why?'

'He claims to have a connection to McDermott and his wife.'

'Rosie? I haven't been able to contact her either.'

'Stuart told us that he and Rosie had known each other for years. They used to be a couple but broke up when Stuart moved to Scotland. It seems that McDermott is the jealous type. He might not be too happy that Stuart was trying to get back into Rosie's life.'

Donna shrugged innocently.

'I don't know anything about that.'

'Are you sure?' Ursula asked sternly. 'For your own sake, Donna, you have to be telling us the truth.'

'I swear I've never heard of him. Besides, what has that got to do with Shiels and then Crossley getting shot? I have to go. If I can't track down McDermott, I'll have to get out of Belfast.'

She got to her feet, but Sidney reached out his hand and suggested that she sit again.

'Let's talk about Sammy Chambers,' he said. 'Ursula, get us some more coffee, please.'

'I don't know anything about Chambers either,' said Donna in alarm. 'What's he got to do with all this?'

'Well,' Sidney replied, 'if you believe that someone local is trying to muscle in on McStay's business interests over here then Chambers is the most likely to be your man.'

'Have you had any contact with him, Donna?' Ursula asked.

Donna looked panic-stricken. She gazed helplessly from Ursula to Sidney.

'I want the truth, Donna,' Sidney warned.

Donna covered her face with both hands and groaned. Then she shook her head defiantly.

'No way! I'm saying nothing more to you pair. You'll get me shot, so you will.'

'You must tell us, Donna. We can't help you otherwise,' said Sidney.

'Nope. No way.'

Sidney winced at Ursula. From her denial, Sidney concluded that Donna was not only frightened of McStay, but she also harboured fears about what Chambers might do to her. Then he switched the subject to Sean Barnes.

They'd been sitting in the flat for more than an hour. Ursula and Sidney were on their second round of pastries to accompany their coffee. Donna settled for another cup of tea and no food.

'How close is Sean to McDermott?' Sidney asked.

'They're not. Like I told you before, Sean is a complete disaster. Everyone knows that, including McDermott.'

'But has Sean worked for him?' Ursula put in.

'Sean worked for Shiels, same as the rest of us.'

Sidney leaned back in his recliner, glancing at his watch. Late afternoons were the worst times for him. He faded badly and usually dozed off after his coffee.

'Donna,' he said, 'you must keep trying to find McDermott. Perhaps if he knows his life is in danger from Owen McStay he'll reach out for help.'

'I can't think of anywhere else to look for him,' said Donna. 'I've tried him at home, I've checked out the pubs he usually drinks in, and I've asked about the town. Nobody has seen or heard from him.'

'Have you tried Sean?'

'I've asked him, but he doesn't know either. If I don't find him soon McStay will come for me instead.'

At that, Donna rose quickly and, without bidding them goodbye, hurried from the flat.

'That woman is at her wits' end, Daddy.'

'Nothing we can do about that.'

'It just occurred to me when we were discussing Chambers. He's another candidate for C in Shiels' diary.'

'Mm, Chambers, Cassidy, Ciaran McDermott or Crossley. Then again it might be our first thought when we found the diary. Coffee.'

'Or cocaine,' said Ursula.

Ursula cleared away the cups and plates while Sidney fell into his longed-for doze. Minutes later he was suddenly wide awake and raring to go.

'Let's go and do some proper work,' he said. 'We have some cases to finish off.'

'No. You're knackered, Daddy. You take it easy for a while. I will go out on my own.'

Sidney didn't argue and Ursula knew that her father was feeling the pace.

Chapter 44

He had only a few days left. If he still wanted his job, Stuart would have to return to Scotland by the start of the following week. He'd spoken to his boss. She'd been quite sympathetic to his situation but could only allow him a few extra days' unpaid leave. With no news forthcoming about Rosie's whereabouts, he reluctantly had given up on his search for the woman he still loved.

Before returning to Scotland, though, he had offered to do some grocery shopping for his parents. They seemed to be growing older and less active with each of his visits. There was no one else close by to help them out. Later today, he planned to take them for a drive to the north coast. Give them a wee treat, he thought, and maybe an overnight stay at a hotel in Portballintrae. He and his dad could spend tomorrow morning on a tour of the distillery in nearby Bushmills.

The Tesco car park at Knocknagoney was busy, but he'd found a space on the far side close to McDonald's yet quite some way from the supermarket entrance. Pushing his trolley loaded with groceries, he became aware of a car slowing behind him. He thought little of it except to make sure he wasn't causing an obstruction for the driver. As he placed shopping bags in the boot of his Volkswagen, he realised that the car had stopped behind him, and he assumed it was about to reverse into a space. When he turned around, however, he saw that the driver of the blue Peugeot had lowered his window. Stuart did not recognise him, but the man was staring right at him.

'Nichol?'

Stuart said nothing but continued to peer at the driver.

'Get in!'

'Who are you? What do you want?'

'If you want to see Rosie, get into the car now! I'm her cousin so hurry up.' The man seemed nervous and looked all around him then back to Stuart.

At the mention of her name, Stuart had no other thought but to do as he was asked. He locked his Volkswagen and climbed into the Peugeot. With a screech of tyres, the car rallied from the shopping centre and was soon speeding through the suburbs.

'Where are we going?' Stuart asked.

The scrawny-looking driver said nothing, keeping his eyes straight ahead.

'Is Rosie all right?'

'Aye, she's grand.'

They travelled along the ring road towards Belmont. Stuart had no idea where they were headed.

'Is she with Ciaran?'

The man didn't reply and kept his eyes dead ahead. Stuart suddenly feared that he wasn't on his way to see Rosie at all.

'That day in the Mournes,' said the driver, breaking his silence, 'how did you get away?'

'You were there?'

The man did not reply.

'Did McDermott send you to get me? Who the hell are you? How do you know Rosie? Why are you asking about the Mournes?'

153

The driver had clammed up again. Stuart felt this was all wrong. This guy was no cousin of Rosie's, and they were not on their way to see her. Somewhere at the end of this journey McDermott would be waiting for him. He had to get out of this car.

'Stop!'

'No way, sunshine.'

The man pressed his foot harder on the accelerator but, as they approached a roundabout, Stuart realised that they would have to slow down to make the turn. Maybe he could escape then. The car slowed, but there was little traffic at the roundabout and they sailed on through. They drove by the entrance to Campbell College and took the exit leading to the busy junction at Knock. Stuart still had no clue to their destination. He waited anxiously for another opportunity to get out of the car.

As they neared the junction, he steeled himself when he saw that the traffic lights were red. At first the driver slowed down but then he seemed to change his mind. As they gathered speed again, Stuart could wait no longer. He seized his chance. He opened the door and tried to step out, but his legs buckled beneath him, and he tumbled from the car. The driver carried on through the red light then swerved to the side of the road, narrowly missing a lorry emerging from the right. Several drivers blared their horns and braked sharply. Eventually, the Peugeot came to a halt at the kerbside. The driver leaned across and pulled the passenger door closed. He glanced behind him, then roared away into the traffic.

Several people rushed from their vehicles to assist the man lying face down in the road.

Chapter 45

The next morning Stuart telephoned Sidney from his bed at the Ulster Hospital. He had sustained cuts and abrasions to his hands, elbows and knees. He'd also suffered a nasty gash to his forehead and had been admitted to a ward for observation for concussion. Sidney listened to his story of escape from a man Stuart claimed he did not know.

'I thought he was taking me to see Rosie, but then he mentioned the Mournes. That's when I realised, he was taking me to McDermott, and I was probably going to be killed.'

'What about the Mournes?' Sidney asked, confused.

There was no answer, and the line went dead.

Ursula came into the lounge from the bathroom, her head wrapped in a towel.

'Who were you talking to?'

Sidney was staring at his mobile and looked puzzled.

'Stuart Nichol.'

'What did he want?'

'He's in hospital. Somebody tried to abduct him yesterday.'

Ursula stopped drying her hair.

'Is he all right?'

Sidney didn't answer. He stood gazing out at the murky lough.

'Daddy? Are you OK?'

She came and stood beside him. It was enough to stir him from his thoughts.

'I've just had a strange conversation with the lad,' he said.

'Strange? In what way?'

'He said that some guy was driving him to see this woman Rosie that he'd told us about. Then Stuart got spooked when the man mentioned the Mournes, so he jumped from the car.'

'Was he hurt?'

'A few scratches and bruises. Possible concussion. But what was it about the Mournes that made him jump from the car? When I asked him, he cut the call.'

When Sidney went for a shower Ursula telephoned Stuart. He sounded sheepish and gave only one-word answers to her questions. Ursula thought it best just to arrange to meet when he got out of hospital. Then perhaps they could discuss things in detail. But Stuart sounded reluctant.

'If you want our help, Stuart then you have to help us. You need to tell us everything.' Ursula was suddenly conscious of having said exactly the same thing to Donna Cassidy the day before.

* * *

The following day they met over lunch at The Dirty Duck, only a few yards from Sidney and Ursula's flat. Sidney was feeling refreshed after a day's rest at home. Ursula couldn't help appearing glad to see Stuart Nichol alive and with only a few scratches on his handsome face.

He told them in detail about his ordeal in the car and of how he made his escape. Sidney, however, was more interested in Stuart's reference to the Mournes.

'Why did you hang up on me? Why did you panic when the driver mentioned the Mournes? Is there something you aren't telling us, son?'

He cleared his throat but still seemed reluctant to explain.

'Come on, Stuart,' Ursula coaxed. 'It's OK, you can trust us. We want to help you find Rosie.'

Ursula's reassurance somehow was enough for him to finally open up.

'The man in the car asked me how I got away from the Mournes. When I asked him if he had been there, he wouldn't answer me. That's when I realised that he must have been involved.'

Sidney and Ursula looked at each other.

'Involved? You need to explain,' said Ursula.

'It was a couple of weeks ago,' Stuart began. 'I just fancied a walk to clear my head. A couple of days before that I'd asked Rosie to leave Ciaran and come to Scotland with me. She turned me down, but I asked her to think about it and told her that I would come and see her before going back. So, I went for a dander in the mountains to mull things over. I had climbed to the Hare's Gap, then onto Slieve Bearnagh and at the top I just sat daydreaming for ages. It was getting late when I started to head back. That's when I spotted three guys coming up the slope. Seemed strange that anyone was making for the summit at that time of the day. It was already getting dark. At first, I thought maybe they were lost, or they were searching for something. Sometimes farmers come looking for their stray sheep. But then when I drew closer, about fifty yards away, they suddenly fanned out. I changed direction and moved to my right just to see how they would react. They quickened their pace. One of them, I was certain, was moving to cut me off. So, I started running. As best as anyone can run across a steep slope covered with heather.'

Stuart dropped his head. He sighed heavily and his hand trembled when he lifted his glass of beer from the table. Ursula placed her hand on his shoulder.

'It's all right, pet. Take your time.'

Stuart managed a few sips of beer. He'd long abandoned his food. Even Sidney had ceased eating.

'I made it into a gully and hoped that they wouldn't follow me. It was getting hard to see in the fading light and for some reason I didn't think these guys looked physically fit, not for plodding over the mountains. I was just beginning to think I'd lost them when this guy leapt from some rocks above me. He landed on top of me, and we tumbled down the gully, through the stream. We must have fallen about twenty feet. Then the guy starts screaming. He'd grabbed hold of me but when we stopped rolling down the gully he let go.

'I scrambled to my feet, but he was writhing in agony in the middle of the stream. I bent over him to see what was wrong and I saw his leg. It was badly broken; his shin bone had pierced his skin and his trousers. He was bleeding heavily. Maybe I should have stayed with him. I panicked. I reckoned that his mates would help him, so I headed on down the gully. It seemed the best way to escape.

'By this time, it was really dark and difficult to pick steps over slippery boulders. But I was careful and took my time. I didn't believe they would still be coming for me. Surely, they would be trying to help their mate. Then I heard what sounded like a gunshot.'

Chapter 46

Sidney and Ursula now realised they were listening to an account of the death of Terry Quinn. The remainder of Stuart's tale might identify the killer.

'I didn't know what to do. I was too frightened to even move and I was freezing cold. I'd got soaked falling down the gully when the guy jumped me.'

'His name was Terry Quinn,' said Sidney.

'I know that now but didn't know it at the time,' Stuart replied.

'Do you know who shot him?' Ursula asked.

She hadn't intended it to sound like an accusation, but Stuart seemed to take it that way.

'It wasn't me! You must believe me. I didn't know these people. It wasn't until later that I even realised they were associated with McDermott.'

'What happened next?' Sidney asked.

'Like I said, I was too scared to move. I just hoped they wouldn't find me. But a few minutes after I heard the shot, maybe longer, I heard voices, and they were getting closer. It was so dark, and I just bolted. They must have only been a few feet from reaching me. I stumbled but I didn't realise I was so close to the reservoir. They must have heard the splash when I fell into the water. It was so cold I couldn't breathe. I knew if I didn't get out, I would die, but I also knew they were standing on the bank directly above me. One of them was calling me by name, but I realised that he couldn't see me. So, I stayed in the water for as long as I could bear the cold. I thought they would never leave. Eventually they gave up calling me, but it felt like hours before I risked climbing out. Thankfully, my rucksack was lying a few yards from where I'd fallen. I tripped over it in the dark. Finding it and getting out of my wet clothes and into my anorak was what saved my life.'

'Did you come across the men again?' Ursula asked.

'No. When I got a bit warmer, I made my way to the dam and then walked down the service road. Took me all night. I called at the park ranger's cottage at Silent Valley and told the man living there that I'd had an accident. He drove me to hospital and then later I made it home. The next day my dad brought me back down to fetch my car.'

'Did you tell the ranger about being attacked?'

He shook his head.

'What about the police?'

'I thought about it, but when I heard on the news that another man's body had been found on the Trassey Track, I just didn't want to get involved. I was worried about Rosie. I was still hoping she would agree to come with me to Scotland. I decided that getting caught up in a police inquiry wouldn't help me convince her.'

'The guys who attacked you,' said Sidney, 'when did you realise they were connected with McDermott?'

'When I was in the water. One of them said Rosie's name as he was searching for me. He warned me to stay away from her.'

'Is it possible that one of them was actually McDermott?' said Ursula.

'I suppose so. I never saw them close up except for the guy who jumped me and broke his leg.'

Sidney had gone quiet. Ursula thought he looked uncomfortable for what Stuart had told them.

'Why didn't you tell us about this sooner?' he said.

'I didn't know if I could trust you. And besides, I don't care about any of it now except for getting Rosie back.'

'Give me one good reason why we should believe your story? What if you are responsible for killing those lads in the mountains because you're obsessed with finding this woman who may not even want to be found by you? She may be perfectly happy with her husband, and you are a dangerous stalker.'

Ursula glared in amazement at her father's candour.

'No! That's not true. I didn't kill anyone. I told you. McDermott is the psycho, not me.' He stood up and attempted to squeeze by Ursula. 'I don't know what I'm doing talking to you. If you can't find McDermott, then you're no help to me.'

Ursula tried to stop him, but Sidney shook his head.

'Daddy? We have to help him.'

Stuart was already making for the door. Ursula looked pleadingly at Sidney. Faced with his incorrigible daughter he quickly relented, and Ursula rushed after Stuart.

* * *

They finished their lunch in silence after Ursula had persuaded Stuart to return. Later they walked back to the flat and Ursula made coffee while Sidney tried to re-engage with the angry young man whom he had earlier accused of being a murderer.

'The man who picked you up, did you recognise him from the Mournes?'

'No.'

'So, it wasn't McDermott driving the car?'

'Absolutely not. I would never have got into the car with McDermott. The man told me he was Rosie's cousin.'

'May have been Sean Barnes,' Ursula piped up. 'You said that he was driving a blue Peugeot. I've seen a car like that parked outside Sean's house in Friendly Street.' Ursula wondered also if Sean had borrowed her white lie when she had claimed to be Taggart's cousin. The man had no imagination.

'Who is he and why would he be doing McDermott's dirty work?' Stuart asked.

'There's a lot more going on than McDermott trying to get at you, son,' said Sidney. 'From what you've just told us, the murder of the two guys in the Mournes is down to McDermott's obsession with you and Rosie. But two more people are dead. We think that has more to do with the kind of business run by Martin Shiels and those who worked for him. Owen McStay is a well-known rogue in Scotland. I think someone, Shiels or perhaps McDermott, has crossed him. He seems intent on finding McDermott just as much as you.'

'I'm looking for him, you're looking for him and now a Scottish gangster is looking for him.'

'That's right. So, we must get to him before anyone else,' said Sidney. 'We're going to need your help, Stuart.'

'I'll do anything to find Rosie.'

'It's dangerous. McDermott is obviously prepared to kill to keep you away from his wife.'

'What he wants is me,' said Stuart.

'Since we believe that it was Sean Barnes who picked you up, it seems likely that he knows where McDermott is hiding.'

'Unless Sean knows nothing and was simply ordered to kill you,' said Ursula. She tried to smile as she said it, but it didn't help.

Stuart suddenly looked alarmed.

'Do you think there's a chance that McDermott doesn't have Rosie, that he's already killed her?' he asked.

All three looked at each other. No one dared consider that possibility.

Chapter 47

Donna spent a sleepless night, sitting by her lounge window, chain-smoking and gazing at an empty street. She was waiting for Sean to come home. According to Valentine when they'd spoken earlier in the day, Sean was the most likely person to know where McDermott was hiding. So, the slimy toerag had been lying to her the whole time.

She had to contact McDermott soon or she was a dead woman. More than her allotted three days had passed. Owen McStay, she'd heard countless times, did not tolerate failure. Not when it came to his money. She knew that even Shiels had at times feared for his life when business ventures did not go to plan. Donna wondered if that was what had really happened. The Crossleys were involved too but did that mean they were acting on orders from McStay, or had they also fallen foul of the Scot? Now she had Sammy Chambers wanting a piece of her. If only she could step aside and allow McStay and Chambers to battle it out. With a bit of luck, the two men would destroy each other, and she would be free to get on with her life.

It was three o'clock in the morning when a car came down the street and stopped outside her front door. She saw that it was Sean. Thank God. She rushed outside before he had the chance to lock himself away in his own house.

'Sean! Where the hell have you been?' Her voice clearly startled him, and he ducked behind his car. 'Sean, it's me for dear sake!'

'Leave me alone, Donna.'

He locked his car and stepped quickly to his front door. She went after him.

'No, you don't, Sean. You are going to tell me where Ciaran is or we're all in the shit, do you hear me, Sean? McStay is gunning for him and if he can't get to him, then he's coming for me. If you don't tell me where McDermott is, I'll point McStay at you!'

'I don't care, Donna. When McDermott finds me, he'll kill me anyway. I messed up badly.'

He opened his door and attempted to go inside, but Donna pushed her way in behind him. She bundled him into his own living room. The place was a disaster; it hadn't been cleaned or tidied in weeks. But nothing else mattered. Not even switching on the lights. Donna shoved him to the sofa and fell on top of him. Sean was a weakling; she easily overcame his resistance.

'Tell me where he is, Sean.'

She sat astride him, slapping his face, back and forth from left to right. The man had little strength to fight back.

'Get off me!'

'Tell me!'

'I can't. He'll kill me.'

'I'm going to kill you if you don't. What the hell do you know that you're too scared to tell me about? Do you know what happened to my Terry? Was it McDermott?'

Her slaps had become punches pounding at Sean's chest and face. He made a flimsy attempt to fend her off. She cried as she thumped at the useless man beneath her. Finally, she grabbed his throat and tried to choke him.

'Get off me!'

With a sudden burst of strength, he pushed Donna off and she tumbled to the floor. Quickly, he sprang to his feet.

'Leave me alone, you fat bitch.'

He kicked her in the side, and she cried out. He kicked her again, but her cries now were met with tears from Sean. He dropped to the floor in a heap beside her.

'What are we going to do, Donna? You have to help me.'

'Tell me where McDermott is,' she begged.

Chapter 48

Sean Barnes' wrist wasn't healing well, and he was failing to take care of it. Driving was awkward, particularly on gear changes. Since early morning, when he'd finally escaped from Donna, he'd parked in a tidy street of terraced houses in Sydenham and waited. Rain and wind lashed against the Peugeot. Another miserable day in Belfast.

It was after ten o'clock when an elderly man emerged from a house, closing his front door behind him. Less than a minute later Stuart Nichol appeared from the same house and soon caught up with the older man. The pair, despite the rain, strolled at a leisurely pace along the street. The younger of the two was the slower on his feet, still nursing injuries from the episode when he'd jumped from a moving vehicle. They were not intending to drive, it seemed. Sean let them go. This was not his opportunity. He slid down in his seat and soon fell asleep.

An hour later, he jerked awake when a delivery van roared along the narrow street. He wiped his eyes and yawned widely. He was thirsty, hungry, and he needed the toilet. Having dozed, he had no idea whether Stuart Nichol had returned home or was still limping around the streets. Fortunately for him, he didn't have to wait long to find out. He watched as, for the second time that morning, Nichol stepped out of the house. This time he walked alone to his green Volkswagen and climbed inside. Sean sat up, gunned his engine and prepared to follow.

The Volkswagen negotiated the narrower streets then, from Station Road, Stuart turned left onto the Holywood Road. Sean had no problem following. But he was much too close.

They had not travelled far before Stuart became aware of the car behind tailgating him. He recognised the blue Peugeot instantly and put his foot down. Sean, impulsive as ever, had no patience to wait for the best opportunity. Despite this section of the Holywood Road being only a single carriageway and heavily constrained by painted lines and bollards, Sean increased his speed then pulled out to overtake the Volkswagen.

Stuart saw the face of the man who had tried to abduct him. He signalled for Stuart to pull over, but there was no way Stuart was submitting. Suddenly, a van approaching from the opposite direction forced the Peugeot to veer towards him. The two cars ran side by side and finally collided before the Volkswagen slewed to the left. Stuart stood on the brakes, but he had little control. In a flash his car bounced over the kerb, swerved further left across the pavement and smashed into the open gate of the Blanchflower Playing Fields. The Peugeot also mounted the pavement but stopped in time to avoid an impact with the metal railings of the park.

Stuart was shaken but uninjured although his airbag had deployed. As he fought to extricate himself from the car, he felt a rush of air as Sean hauled the driver's door open.

'Get out, Nichol.'

Stuart offered no resistance, not when faced by an enraged man wielding a gun. He clambered slowly from his car and could only hope that somebody would come to his aid. Passing vehicles slowed and drivers looked on, but none of them stopped.

'Into my car. You can drive,' Sean commanded. 'Try another stunt like the other day and I'll put a bullet in your head, understand me?'

Stuart said nothing and did as he was instructed. His head was spinning, his body shaking. Sean got into the passenger seat and flashed his gun once again at his quarry.

'Drive.'

Chapter 49

Donna had fallen asleep on the couch once Sean had fled. She was exhausted and frightened. As soon as she gathered her strength, she would go to see McDermott, try to talk some sense into him. He'd caused a hell of a lot of trouble and if she didn't produce him or at least find out what he was up to, then Owen McStay was going to hurt her badly. She would never serve McDermott on a plate to the Scot. He had been a friend and he didn't deserve that. She would have to plead with him to contact McStay and explain himself. And she would do it all without a word to Sidney Valentine. He was a complication she could do without. Besides, she had yet to figure out exactly what the man was up to. Was he really working for the cops? Or did he stick his nose into other people's business just for the hell of it? And that daughter of his really creeped her out.

She smoked the last of her cigarettes then returned to her own house and went upstairs for a shower. As she finished dressing, she heard the doorbell sound. Her heart raced. Surely it wasn't McStay. Maybe Sean had contacted McDermott and he'd come to see her. She hurried downstairs, fiddling with her bra strap beneath her tunic. Two figures were visible in the dawn light. Neither one looked happy to be there. Her hand trembled as she opened her door.

'Morning, Donna,' said Haig looking alert and business-like, except for her hair blowing around in the stiff breeze. 'We've come for your news.'

'News?'

McCord barged inside, ushering Donna backwards as he went. Haig followed, closing the door behind her. By the time they entered the lounge Donna was under a firm grip, McCord's hand at her throat.

'McDermott, where is he?' Haig demanded.

'Owen said I had three days,' Donna struggled to get the words out. Her hands went helplessly to McCord's as he applied more pressure to her neck.

'You've had more than three days, pet, and we don't have the patience that Owen has,' Haig said, looking around the room. Her eyes lit on the dining table and chairs by the rear window. She lifted one metal-framed chair and placed it in the centre of the room.

McCord forced Donna downwards and she more fell than sat on it.

'I haven't been able to contact him yet. I was hoping–'

McCord slapped her hard on the face with the back of his hand and she cried out.

'Wrong answer,' he said.

He stepped to the rear window and pulled hard on the drawstrings of the vertical blind. Then he produced a penknife from his pocket, opened it and cut the string away from its mooring. Using two of the strands, he tied Donna's hands separately to the chair frame. While McCord worked, Haig ventured to the kitchen. Donna tried to plead with the young man.

'Please. Give me till the end of the day. I promise I'll get McDermott for you. Just don't hurt me.'

'It's not me you have to worry about, hen.'

Haig returned holding a roll of duct tape, a knife and two lemons. Donna didn't think it looked good although she had no idea what was about to happen.

'I like a house that's well equipped with essentials,' said Haig with a malicious smile.

She placed the knife and lemons on the sofa then peeled off a strip of tape, handing it to McCord.

'One more time before we start, Donna love,' she said. 'Where the hell is McDermott?'

Donna shook her head, her eyes flooding with tears, her cheek still burning from the slap meted out by McCord. Haig nodded. McCord stuck the tape across Donna's mouth. Then he walked from the room and closed the door behind him.

'Men, eh? Big wooses. Can't stand the sight of blood.'

Donna struggled to get free, the dining chair rocking on the floor.

'Easy on, Donna. I haven't done anything yet.'

Haig lifted the small but, as Donna was aware, sharp knife and held it up, inspecting its blade.

'Now, all you have to do, pet, is nod your wee head or blink those beautiful dark eyes when you are ready to tell me where McDermott is. Soon as you're ready to talk I'll stop what I'm doing, OK?'

Chapter 50

Rosie was awakened before dawn by the wind buffeting the slate roof of the cottage. Every gap seemed to channel the draught, and as the rain found its way in, it dripped and formed several puddles on the floor. She shivered from the cold. Connor snuggled close beside her, sapping the heat from her body.

Breakfast had been set into their room each morning although the time varied, she guessed, because Ciaran seemed to sleep late. He did not leave the cottage as often as he had when they had first come here. Their attempted escape, it seemed, had made him more cautious. In the evenings he went to fetch their takeaway food that now consisted only of fish or sausages with chips.

She and Connor had been ill with loose bowels and several episodes of vomiting. The room held the stench of their discomfort. She had to scream at the top of her voice just to get Ciaran to come and empty the commode. She'd given up hope of escape and could only pray for rescue. She was past caring about her or Connor's filthy condition. Her time was spent trying to keep warm and listening for every movement within the house.

She wondered about Stuart. Would Ciaran really bring him here? That's what he'd told her. And what then? It was stretching matters to believe that her husband would then simply let them go. She couldn't decide if Ciaran was capable of murder, but then again it was hearing about the death of Martin Shiels that had prompted her to flee their home in Twinbrook in the first place. Somehow, she knew that Ciaran was involved; he and Martin had been friends. But was her husband the killer or was he fearing for his own life from whoever had murdered Martin Shiels?

The rain and wind hadn't let up but, in the early morning, she'd heard a noise outside. Car doors closed. There were shouts. Angry shouts. She heard the door of the cottage open and then, perhaps caught by the wind, it banged against the wall. The voices became muted when the visitors moved indoors. Rosie couldn't make out what was being said. One of them had to be Ciaran but there were at least two others.

She went to the window and peered out. There was nothing to see but pouring rain and the long grass swaying in the gale. She hardly dared to breathe as she strained her ears to listen for spoken words. Who had come to see

Ciaran? Were they here to get Connor and her out of this hovel? She pressed her ear to the door and felt the cold air squeezing through the crack. Connor rose from the bed and came to his mother's side.

'What's the matter, Mummy?'

'Sssh, Connor. I'm listening for your daddy, pet.'

'Can we go home now?'

She placed her hand on his head and pulled him close.

'I hope so, darling. I really do.'

Chapter 51

Sidney and Ursula waited all morning to hear from Stuart Nichol. Ursula tried calling his mobile but there was no reply. Their plan was to have Stuart confirm that Sean Barnes was the man who had tried to abduct him. Assuming that it had been Sean, they intended to follow him in the hope he would eventually lead them to Ciaran McDermott. Without Stuart, however, they would have to assume that Sean was indeed their man and follow him anyway.

They avoided a tailback on the Sydenham bypass by staying on the Holywood Road. Had they been passing an hour earlier they would have encountered the confrontation between Sean and Stuart at the gates to the Blanchflower Playing Fields. As they drove by, they failed to notice Stuart's abandoned Volkswagen by the park's entrance.

On their way to Friendly Street, they called at the Nichol family home in Sydenham, but Stuart's mother told Ursula that her son had already gone out.

* * *

Donna Cassidy's Volvo sat outside her home but there was no sign of a blue Peugeot that they believed belonged to Sean Barnes. Instead, parked next to the Volvo, was a metallic-gold Lexus. As Sidney and Ursula were getting out of their van, a man and a woman hurried from Donna's house, jumped into the Lexus and sped away.

'Who do you think they were?' Ursula asked.

'They work for Owen McStay,' Sidney replied, recalling his encounter with the pair in the subway.

Ursula stared quizzically at her father.

Without further explanation, he said, 'I'll check if Sean is at home, you call with Donna.'

Sidney got no reply from knocking on Sean's front door. Ursula had no response from Donna's. They stepped to the side and peered through the respective lounge windows of each house.

'Donna looks in a bad way, Daddy.'

She tried the door handle. It wasn't locked and she rushed into the living room.

'Oh my God! Donna, what happened?'

The young woman was hardly recognisable as the person who'd sat with them in their flat a few days earlier. Blood covered her body from her head to her ankles. There were numerous cuts on her torso, arms, legs, and neck. Her wrists were firmly tied to a chair and her head hung to one side. Ripped clothing lay in a pile on the floor beside her. Ursula carefully peeled the tape from Donna's mouth.

'Donna, love!' she cried. 'Speak to me.'

Sidney telephoned for an ambulance, while Ursula grabbed kitchen roll and used it to stem the flow of blood from those cuts that were bleeding profusely. All the while, she tried to get a response from a semi-conscious Donna.

'The ambulance is on its way, love. You'll be all right.'

Ursula knelt beside the chair, her knee squeezing a slice of lemon into the carpet.

'What the hell is this?'

Donna groaned; her eyes opened slightly. She tried to say something, but her voice was weak, and her words were jumbled.

'Don't worry, Donna, we'll get whoever did this to you.'

'C... Ciaran. Help.'

'Ciaran?' Ursula asked, as she continued to soak up blood from Donna's body.

Sidney found the knife used by Haig on the floor and cut the cords binding Donna's hands to the chair. The slightest movement induced agonising cries from the woman.

'I wish that ambulance would hurry up,' said Ursula, upset by the injuries inflicted on the woman. 'Seems like they squeezed lemon juice into those cuts. That has to sting.'

'Dromara,' Donna slurred following a bout of painful cries. 'Help Ciaran.'

'Is that where he is, Dromara?' Ursula asked.

Donna managed to nod once.

'Where is Sean?' Ursula asked.

There was no reply. Saliva and blood spewed from her mouth.

'Whereabouts in Dromara? Can you tell us, Donna?' Sidney asked.

An ambulance pulled up outside and Ursula greeted the two paramedics, explaining what they had found and suggesting they contact the police once Donna had been transferred to hospital.

'Did you get any more information?' Ursula asked Sidney as they hurried back to their van.

'She mentioned something about Dundrum.'

'Do you not mean Dromara?'

'She also said Dundrum,' Sidney replied.

'Which is it, Dundrum or Dromara?'

Before driving off, Ursula checked Google Maps on her phone. After a few seconds she set it down and started the engine.

'How about Dundrum Road, Dromara?' she said.

'That narrows it down a bit. Let's get out there, it's all we've got. McStay's people must be on their way there too.'

Chapter 52

Sean couldn't help his delight when he jumped from his car to be met by Ciaran McDermott standing in the porch of the cottage.

'I got him, Ciaran! I got Nichol for you!'

McDermott glared at the figure sitting behind the wheel of the Peugeot. Stuart glared back.

'Get him in here.'

Sean opened the driver's door and pointed the gun at Stuart.

'Out!'

Stuart eased himself from the car. He was stiff now, feeling pain in his neck and shoulders from the collision on the Holywood Road compounded by his injuries when he'd jumped from the Peugeot days earlier. Only the thought that he might at last see Rosie kept him upright. Sean gripped his arm and shunted him in the direction of the cottage door. McDermott had already gone back inside. Stuart took in his surroundings as best he could. It was an old farmyard that seemed disused. Beside the cottage stood a small barn, whitewashed with a huge cartwheel, at one time painted red and white but now badly weathered, resting against the wall. Next to the Peugeot sat a red Mazda and beyond that was another whitewashed barn with a red door. The gravelled yard was overrun with grass and weeds.

Sean pushed Stuart inside then followed, slamming the door behind him. In the bare kitchen, McDermott stood warming himself by a log fire.

'Well, Nichol, it's been a while. I hope you like the place. It's just a rental but I think it's homely.'

'Where's Rosie? What have you done with her?'

'Fair play to you. It didn't take you long to think of her.'

McDermott examined the face of his long-time rival. Stuart looked frightened but brave enough to speak his truth.

'Good news for you, too,' said McDermott, 'she's made her choice. I asked her the other day and she told me that she wants to be with you, can you believe it?'

'I want to see her. You've no right to keep me from seeing her.'

'I've every right! She's *my* wife!'

Sean suddenly put the pistol to the back of Stuart's head.

'Will I waste him now, Ciaran?'

'Don't be stupid. He wants to see Rosie. Take him upstairs. And leave that gun here. I don't want you scaring young Connor.'

Sean barged Stuart towards the narrow staircase. McDermott smiled menacingly as their eyes met. He was taller than Stuart and had a strong athletic build. He had been an accomplished Gaelic footballer in the days before his insecurity over Rosie had festered to become an obsession. His face displayed a lifetime of hardship. As Stuart had always believed, it lacked any genuine charm.

Sean unlocked the bedroom door and pushed it open wide. He stood back and motioned for Stuart to enter. Rosie was waiting on the other side.

'Stuart!'

'Rosie! Are you alright?'

He rushed forwards and took her in his arms. Rosie lost hold of the duvet cover wrapped around her; it slipped to the floor revealing her filthy clothing.

Sean appeared to savour the vision of the beautiful yet bedraggled woman. Then he slammed the door and slotted the bolt into place.

'What do we do now, Ciaran?' Sean asked when he came downstairs.

McDermott held a mug of tea in his left hand. He sat calmly at the table as Sean stood over him.

'I could murder a cup of tea,' Sean chirped. 'Haven't had anything since last night.'

'You can go home now. I don't need you for anything.'

Sean was about to help himself to the teapot, but now he suddenly looked awkward and at a loss for what to do or say next.

'You need to get out of this place, soon, Ciaran,' he warned in a shaky voice.

'Why is that?'

'People are looking for you. It might not be safe here.'

'What people?'

With hands trembling, Sean poured some tea into a stained mug then lifted a carton of milk from the table.

'Donna wants to see you.'

'Don't worry about her. I can handle her later. Anybody else?'

Sean glanced towards his boss but failed to look him in the face. His hands were shaking so much he could hardly raise the mug to his mouth.

'Donna told me that Owen McStay was over. He wants to find out what's been happening, after Shiels and that.'

'Have you told anyone where I am, Sean?'

Sean didn't answer. He lowered his head.

'Sean?'

'I might have said something to Donna.'

'You're an arse, Sean. She'll tell McStay, and they'll come for me. I told you to keep your mouth shut. If you'd just done what I asked instead of cocking it all up.'

'I'm sorry, Ciaran.'

'You're a liability, Sean.'

McDermott suddenly reached for the pistol that Sean had left on the table while he'd gone upstairs. But Sean got to it first, his mug of tea bouncing on the table and splashing over McDermott's legs. He pointed the gun at his boss.

'I'm sorry I messed up, Ciaran. I did my best, honest I did.'

McDermott raised his hands and smiled.

'Come on, Sean mate. You're not going to use that thing on me. Not after all we've been through.'

Sean's hand trembled as he continued to point the gun at McDermott. But he was holding it with his sprained and still painful wrist.

They stared at each other, but McDermott, still grinning, showed no fear. Suddenly, he reached again for the gun. Sean fired once.

Chapter 53

Rosie screamed and clutched at Stuart. Connor hugged them both.

'It's all right, pet,' said Rosie.

'We have to get out of here.' Stuart pulled on the door handle in vain. 'Ciaran!' he shouted.

An uncomfortable silence had fallen over the cottage. Neither Stuart nor Rosie dared imagine what had happened when they'd heard the shot from the kitchen below. All activity downstairs seemed to have stopped.

There were no voices. They'd heard the front door open with a bang, but no one had left by car.

'He has to let us go,' said Stuart, more to encourage Rosie. 'Surely, he knows that now.'

Rosie sobbed into his shoulder. She held on to the man she had always loved. That much was so obvious now. She would die here rather than let him go again.

A short while later, the bolt was released, and McDermott kicked the door open wide. Stuart jumped up from the bed ready to defend Rosie. He was faced with the broad-shouldered McDermott holding a baseball bat.

'Please, Ciaran,' Rosie pleaded. 'Let us go now. We can all have a fresh start. We're all to blame, but we can put it behind us.'

'Nice wee thought, my sweet little Rosie. But too late, my darling. Stuart here messed it all up when he first came into your life. And he spoiled everything for us when he came back.'

'Ciaran, I only want what is best for Rosie and Connor,' said Stuart.

'Shut up! You don't get to say anything. I've one question for my wife, that's all.'

Rosie's eyes were wide and sparkled with her tears. She trembled before her husband but still held on to the arm of the man she loved.

'Well, Rosie love. Who's it going to be? I'm asking you for the last time.'

She lowered her head and sobbed. It was all the answer McDermott needed.

'In that case, I'll bid you goodbye, my lovely.'

'Daddy?' said Connor, held tightly by his mother yet trying to reach for the only man he had known as his father.

McDermott didn't answer.

'Ciaran! Please, let us go. Please!' Rosie fell to her knees and wept.

McDermott swung the bat to keep Stuart at bay then made a hasty retreat. He bolted the door again when he left.

Stuart tried to comfort Rosie, and for a short time there were only the sounds of her sobbing. Then a shattering fear suddenly gripped them. They heard a sloshing sound and the unmistakable smell of petrol swept under the door.

'Please, Ciaran!'

Chapter 54

The Dundrum Road at Dromara was nearly four and a half miles long until it joined the Drumkeeragh Road. Sidney and Ursula had no idea of the exact address or indeed if this road was the place where McDermott was to be found. Fortunately, it was a rural district, with only scattered farms and isolated bungalows. There were relatively few properties, although it seemed they would have to check each one until they found their man.

As Ursula drove the van along Dundrum Road, Sidney made several phone calls. It was high time that the police became involved in this hunt. More lives were at risk.

They had only Donna's mumbled instruction to work from. Despite her injuries she had been eager that Sidney and Ursula should get to McDermott quickly. Haig and her sidekick McCord had had a head start but hopefully were less familiar with the location, and there was a chance that Donna had been even less explicit when she told them. Sidney and Ursula were well into their exploration by the time the Scots had wandered aimlessly through Dromara and only by a fluke had turned onto the Dundrum Road.

In his phone call to DCI Harvey, Sidney alerted the detective to a gold Lexus, informing him that its Scottish occupants were responsible for a horrific attack on a woman from Friendly Street in Belfast.

Ursula had already driven the entire length of the Dundrum Road without seeing anything to arouse their suspicion.

'If McDermott is hiding along here, Daddy, you would imagine that the property must be well out of sight of the road.'

'We'll just have to follow each of these lanes right to the end and hope that if he is skulking in a farmhouse, he doesn't see us coming. We don't want him running off just as we find him.'

Ursula turned the car around where the Dundrum Road entered the centre of Dromara village and headed back to open countryside. Several farm buildings sat on the brow of a hill to their right. They found them deserted with only a tractor parked next to a hay barn. Another lane on the opposite side of the road ran into the distance, rising and falling over several hillocks. They were about to enter it until Ursula alerted Sidney to a plume of dark smoke rising in the distance.

'Leave this one,' said Sidney. 'Let's have a look at where that smoke is coming from.'

Ursula pressed her foot harder on the accelerator and a minute later they had drawn level with the source of the smoke. Despite the wind and rain, it was obvious that a significant fire was in progress. Thick black smoke furled into the grey sky.

'That's not a mere burning of rubbish, there must be a building on fire,' said Sidney. 'I hope we're not too late.'

They noticed that the lane to their left had a closed gate. It was well overgrown at the entrance, easy to miss for someone driving by at speed. Sidney jumped out, and after a brief struggle with the rusted bolt, he managed to swing the gate inwards. Ursula drove into the lane and waited for Sidney to rejoin her in the van. Ahead of them was a lane dotted with potholes filled with water. The heavy rain of the morning had not abated.

The laneway swept over a rise and then veered downwards to the left. The volume of smoke had increased by the time the Valentines could see its source. Flames surged from an old cottage sending sparks upwards and swirling in the gale. Ursula drove the van as far as she could then stopped in the yard a safe distance from the cottage. The searing heat warmed the billowing wind as they stepped from the van. The cottage was well ablaze.

Standing in the yard, hands by his sides, admiring his handy work was a man they assumed to be McDermott.

'Is anyone still inside?' Ursula shouted above the crackle and roar of the inferno.

McDermott turned to face her. At first, he seemed bemused by her presence and made no reply until Ursula called him by name.

'Ciaran! Who's in there?'

'Who the hell are you?'

Chapter 55

McDermott stepped in Sidney's way as he made for the house.

'Clear off. This has nothing to do with you.' He grabbed Sidney by the arm.

'We know all about it, sunshine,' Sidney shouted as he tried to free himself from the man's grasp.

Ursula rushed to her father's aid and scraped her boot down McDermott's right shin. He cried out in pain but also lost his grip of Sidney.

'Is Rosie in there, Ciaran? And Stuart?' Sidney barked his questions.

'Who are you people?' McDermott had stooped to massage his leg.

Sidney rushed to the open door of the cottage. Flames and smoke swirled in the hallway. He could get no further. The window to the side of the front door suddenly cracked then shattered in the heat and flames escaped. He could hear cries from somewhere within. Moving to the left, he attempted to make his way around the side of the building, but it was a long detour because of the attached barn. At the rear he peered through a downstairs window. The fire was in full swing on the ground floor and the ceiling was alight. Sidney heard more cries from within the house. Moving to the gable end, he now stood below a small first-floor window. He could just make out activity within the room.

Stuart was battering the commode against the window in a desperate effort to get out. Smoke was filling the room and flames had already taken hold at the door. The floor was soon likely to crash into the kitchen below, and they would be lost. He had broken the glass panes but was struggling to dislodge the window frame. Once more he rammed the commode at the frame and some of the old wood splintered. Rosie squatted close by clutching her son. They held the old duvet to their mouths, but the smoke was gradually overpowering them.

'Stay close to the window,' Sidney called to Stuart. 'I'll get you out.'

Ursula somehow had to stop McDermott from going after her father. He was a tall and well-built man. She would never win if she had to wrestle with him. Her first attempts were easily shrugged off as he pushed her to the ground and kicked her in the side. While Ursula languished trying to draw breath McDermott bounded after Sidney.

The door to one of the barns was unlocked and Sidney peered inside for something to help him rescue the people trapped in the cottage. He spied an old pair of step ladders stacked in a corner. The floor was strewn with pieces of farm equipment including an old plough and several wooden chicken crates. Sidney had to pick his way through to reach the ladders.

Ursula scrambled to her feet and saw McDermott making for the open door of the barn. Ignoring the sharp pain in her side, she hurried to the rear door of her van and opened it. When she turned towards the barn, she held a crossbow in her hands.

McDermott snatched the stepladders from Sidney's grasp when he tried to leave the barn. In the struggle Sidney was thrown to the floor. As McDermott prepared to smash the ladders down on her father Ursula fired her weapon. The bolt lodged deep in the man's right thigh, and he stumbled away before crashing to the ground still holding the ladders.

'I'll have those,' said Sidney when he clambered to his feet.

He pulled the ladders from the stricken McDermott and hurried back to the window where Stuart was still trying to break free, but the ladders did not reach all the way up when opened. Quickly, Sidney returned to the barn and found a length of wooden baton that he hoped would be sturdy enough to dislodge the window frame.

On his return, he saw that Stuart had now succeeded in removing most of it. Just one horizontal piece was intact. Sidney climbed up the ladders and wedged his strip of wood between the windowsill and the remaining crosspiece of the frame. Steadying himself, he pulled hard on the wood. The last piece of frame splintered and finally came away.

Ursula approached McDermott and noted her handiwork with the crossbow, an extra skill she had acquired from her nights at archery club.

'I'll give you a hand if you like, Ciaran.'

'Who the hell are you?' was all he could say as he wheezed in pain. He tried to sit upright.

'Bit of a cliché, mate, but you could say we're your worst nightmare.'

Stooping down, she grasped his left wrist and swept it behind his back. Then she pulled upwards in a lock to entice him to his feet. His wrist would break if McDermott did not immediately stand. He had no choice. Struggling to his feet, he cried out in pain when he applied weight to his wounded leg.

'Walk this way,' said Ursula.

She continued to force his wrist upwards, and he groaned as she directed him to the van. Once there, she took hold of the bolt in his thigh and pushed it further into his flesh. McDermott yelled in excruciating pain. While he trembled from the shock, Ursula quickly bound his hands with cable ties that they kept in the van and, despite his efforts to resist, she also secured his feet.

'Lie down, Ciaran love, you need to rest now.'

With a hefty shove, Ursula successfully landed her prisoner, doubled over with pain, into the back of the van. She gathered his legs and feet and tucked them in. McDermott bawled like an aggrieved toddler with each movement. She pulled a length of duct tape from a roll within the van and stuck it over his mouth. When he was secure, Ursula gave the bolt in his thigh another wiggle. McDermott's body shuddered but with his mouth taped his cries were muted.

'That'll keep you occupied for a while. For your sake, I hope Stuart and your wife make it OK.'

She slammed the door and was going to help her father when a car rolled into the yard and stopped beside her. It was the gold Lexus she had seen earlier outside Donna's house. The driver lowered his window.

'What's going on?' McCord asked.

'Really?' Ursula replied, incredulously. 'I would say there's a house on fire.'

Haig jumped out of the car.

'Where's Ciaran?' she called as Ursula hurried on.

'Don't know any Ciaran,' said Ursula. 'There's a family in need of rescuing.' She ran off to help Sidney.

Flames and smoke bellowed from every opening of the cottage. Ursula held the ladders steady as Sidney scrambled down holding Connor over his shoulder. Rosie was next to emerge, but for a few seconds Ursula lost sight of Stuart. She took Connor from Sidney who then turned to help Rosie.

Suddenly a loud crash and a fresh whoosh of flame belched from the front of the cottage. Stuart yelled for help. Having taken only a single step down the ladders Rosie jumped and landed on Sidney who thumped heavily to the ground.

'Stuart!' Ursula cried out.

From within the thick smoke hands appeared and gripped at the windowsill. Then the struggling figure emerged from the room just as the floor crashed into the kitchen below. Finally, he clambered onto the stepladders and descended unsteadily to be met, firstly with a hug from Ursula followed by one from Rosie. Ursula then stepped away to check on Sidney.

'Where's Ciaran?' Rosie asked, fearfully.

'He ran off,' said Ursula. 'He was too quick for me.'

Haig and McCord were now looking on.

'But you said you didn't know Ciaran,' McCord snapped.

'I lied, what can I say?'

The group of seven people stepped further back from the raging fire but still enduring the wind and rain. The cottage was all but lost.

'Anyone else inside?' Sidney asked. He had noticed the blue Peugeot parked next to the red Mazda.

'The guy I told you about,' Stuart said, coughing profusely. 'He brought me here. I think McDermott may have shot him, but I don't know where he is.'

'If he is in there, we can't help him now,' said Sidney, his hand raised to feel the heat radiating from the inferno.

Ursula left them briefly and returned with two bottles of water that she handed to Rosie and Stuart.

'Take a drink,' she said. 'Ambulance, police and fire service are on their way. Stuart, you, Rosie and Connor wait here. Daddy, we'll have to move the van out of the way for the emergency services. And we can go after that McDermott fella, see where he's got to.' She winked at Sidney.

Haig and McCord were already getting back into the Lexus. They would have difficulty driving away, however. When Ursula had gone to fetch the bottles of water, she had let the air out of the rear tyres on their car. Ursula giggled when she noticed McCord banging his hands on the steering wheel when he realised something was up with his car.

She waved playfully at the big Scot before driving away with Sidney and their captured guest. As they trundled down the lane, a fire engine waited by the gate for them to exit. Behind a second fire engine Sidney and Ursula saw DCI Harvey in a car within a line of police vehicles. Ursula drew alongside and lowered her window. Harvey, looking perplexed, lowered his also.

'Hiya, Corp! Down that lane you'll find the people who tortured Donna Cassidy. They're having a spot of bother with their motor. Oh, and a couple with a child need medical attention. They'll tell you the rest. See ya!'

'Wait! Where the hell are you pair going?'

Harvey was too late. Ursula roared the van along the country road.

Chapter 56

Tyrella Beach is no place to be in violent weather. During a warm summer it's a beautiful spot for picnics, barbecues, paddling in the sea and playing football on the sand. It is also one of those rare places in Northern Ireland where a vehicle may venture beyond any car park to sit on the long strand.

Ursula drove through the gates, along the drive and onto the deserted beach. Immediately, she turned right and motored as far as she thought was wise from the entrance. She was wily enough to know that she shouldn't go too close to the water's edge. Many a one had to be rescued when their vehicle became surrounded by the Irish Sea.

The reason for using a van rather than a car in connection with their business was more apparent on these occasions. In addition to their injured passenger skulking in the back, was Ursula's crossbow for when the need arose, two longbows, a saloon-style wooden chair, a spade, a shovel and a shelf stocked with items including torches, duct tape, cable ties, bottled water and several packets of biscuits.

McDermott was conscious but clearly in distress from the wound to his thigh, something that Ursula continued to exploit until she had him placed in her desired position.

Sidney was well muffled in his outdoor clothing: heavy jumper, anorak, bobble hat and scarf. Ursula was less heavily clothed as she still had some manual work to do.

'Who are you people?' McDermott asked for the umpteenth time since they had peeled the tape from his mouth. He had yet to receive a satisfactory answer. He had been secured to the saloon chair and placed on the sand, the wind thrashing the rain into his face. He couldn't see them in the dark but knew from painful experience that they were still there.

'What do you want with me?'

Sidney leaned on the bonnet of the van between the headlights that not only glared in McDermott's face but also provided light for Ursula who was digging in the sand behind him.

'Where are the police? Are you not going to hand me over to them?'

'In answer to your first question, Ciaran. My name is Sidney and that's my daughter Ursula. The company name is SV Solutions.'

'Never heard of you.'

'Not important.'

McDermott struggled on the seat. He'd suddenly become aware of Ursula's activity behind him. His hands and feet remained bound, and a rope held him to the chair. The bolt from the crossbow still protruded from his thigh.

'As for your second question,' Sidney continued, 'I thought the answer was obvious. I want you to explain why you murdered four people and tried to kill several more, including your wife.'

'None of your business. Just get me to the cops, I'll explain everything to them. I'm not talking to you psychos.'

'He's not a very nice man, Daddy,' Ursula called out. She was already knee-deep in the hole.

'Let's start with Shane Taggart and Terry Quinn,' said Sidney, his arms folded. 'Why did you kill them?'

McDermott didn't answer.

'How's the digging going, love?' Sidney asked.

Their prisoner tried to peer over his shoulder.

'Not bad, Daddy. It'll be easy to get it nice and deep.'

'You two are loopers. You'll never get away with this. Besides, you're not scaring me.'

He didn't notice Ursula pause her digging and step from the trench. She placed her hand on the bolt lodged in his thigh and he yelled in agony as she twisted it.

'You need to learn some manners, talking to my daddy like that. Now behave yourself and answer the questions.'

'Why Taggart and Quinn?' Sidney repeated.

McDermott writhed in pain but seemed to have got the message from Ursula.

'That was Sean Barnes. Useless twat! I sent the three of them to finish off Nichol for me. Make it look like an accident. That was all they had to do. They followed him into the Mournes. Sean told me that Quinn fell and broke his leg when he jumped Nichol. So, the eejit shot him, because he didn't think there was any way to get him help for his busted leg.'

'What about Taggart?' Sidney asked.

'Sean topped him because he'd witnessed what had happened to Quinn. The worst part was that in the end they didn't even get Nichol. He turned up a day later sniffing round my Rosie.'

'Thank you. That's all I wanted to know. Are you nearly ready, Ursula? It's miserable out here.'

'Not long now, Daddy.' She had all but disappeared within the trench.

McDermott wriggled furiously on the chair, but he was unable to get free, and merely exacerbated the pain in his thigh.

'Hold on a minute,' he said. 'Do you not want to know about Martin Shiels?'

'Not really,' Sidney replied. 'I assume you either went to ask Shiels for money, he refused, and you shot him, or you sent Sean to rob him, and he cocked that one up as well.'

'I needed money to get away. To start over with or without Rosie. Nichol had pestered her after those eejits messed up in the Mournes. If she decided to go away with him, I was going to end them both and then clear off. Shiels wasn't supposed to die.'

'Why get Sean to do your bidding?'

'He was an easy touch. Sean liked to think he was the big guy on the rise. Promise him something and he would do whatever I asked him to do. He actually believed that he was my right-hand man, and we were going to topple Shiels and take on McStay. Total eejit.'

'Desmond Crossley. I suppose Sean made a better job of that.'

'How do you know about the Crossleys? Are you working for McStay?'

'Nearly finished, Daddy.'

'Hold on! Wait! You can't do this. You have to hand me over to the cops.'

'No, we don't,' Sidney replied.

'But Sean did all the killing. I've just told you. It wasn't me!'

'Tell me, was it worth taking all those lives just to soothe your jealousy?'

'What do you want me to say?'

'Why kill Desmond Crossley? What did he have to do with your beef with Stuart Nichol?'

Ciaran shook his head in despair.

'That was down to Sean. In his stupid twisted head, he decided that Crossley was a danger to us because we had worked for Shiels. He took him out before he could tell the cops anything.'

'What did you do with Susan?'

Ciaran laughed.

'Nothing, honest to God. She came to the house the day Shiels got shot. She had been robbing us all the whole time, including McStay. Shiels knew about it, but the pair of them were intending to get out of the country together. He told me that they'd taken about two million from McStay. I never clapped eyes on Susan. Ask Sean, he'll tell you.'

'He's still alive?' Sidney asked, surprised by the information.

'He tried to kill me at the cottage, but the daft eejit couldn't shoot straight with his busted wrist. The bullet missed me and lodged in the mantelpiece. So, he took off across the fields. Then you lot showed up and spoiled my fun.'

'You've made life very complicated for yourself,' said Sidney. 'Why keep your wife a prisoner?'

'Once Shiels was dead I knew that the cops and McStay would come looking for me. I didn't want Nichol taking her, so I brought Connor and her to the cottage. Only temporary. Once I finally got my hands on Nichol, I was going to finish them all and clear off.'

'How are you getting on, love?'

'I think that should be deep enough.' Ursula climbed from the trench, brushing sand from her clothes.

'Please don't kill me. I'll tell the cops the truth. I'll tell them everything. I have money. I can pay you. A hundred grand and you let me go. It's McStay's money, serves him right. I found it in Shiels' house.'

'It doesn't work like that,' said Sidney.

'Why not? Everybody has a price. A hundred grand and you can still hand me over to the cops. How about that?'

'You see, Ciaran, I am a man interested in justice, proper justice. A hundred thousand pounds is not much for the lives of four people. Twenty-five grand a head. A pittance, don't you think? And what about your wife? You also tried to kill her and her son. I've seen too many killers handed a life sentence that turns out to be only fifteen years, sometimes even less than that. Doesn't seem right to me. And then, in prisons like Maghaberry, they're treated to three meals a day, a warm cell, free education, gym, library, dentist and hairdresser. Some of them when they get released with their degree from the Open University get jobs where they end up telling the rest of us how to live our lives. It's just not fair. Where's the justice for the victims and their families? What would you say is a fair price for the taking of a life?'

McDermott didn't reply. His head dropped to his chest, and he mumbled to himself.

Sidney removed his dark glasses from the pocket of his anorak and put them on.

'What music would you like, Daddy?'

'Help me! Somebody!' McDermott bawled into the darkness. 'Please! Don't kill me!'

'Calm your flaps, Ciaran,' said Ursula. She saw McDermott's face riven with fear. 'Just tell us the truth. Sean didn't kill anyone, did he? I mean, the guy's a complete loser, couldn't organise the proverbial piss-up. Can't even make decent chips. Besides, you've just told us that you stole money from Shiels' house. It was you, not Sean, who was there that day, and it was you who killed him. And it was you who messed up in the Mournes.'

Ursula lifted her spade, swung it through the air, ready to swipe at Ciaran's head.

'OK! OK! I killed them all,' McDermott wept. 'Taggart and Quinn were useless, even worse than Sean. Laurel and Hardy wouldn't be in it.'

'What about Shiels?' Sidney asked.

'He wouldn't give me any money. That's when he told me about his plan to run away with Susan. Then he told me I was sacked, so I blew his head off. I found a hundred grand in a bag in his office, so I helped myself. Susan came in, found Shiels, freaked out and then made a run for it. I was about to go as well but somebody else came into the house, so I hid in the utility room at the back.'

'And Desmond Crossley?'

'Like I said, he was likely to tell the cops about all of us working for McStay. I thought I could lay the blame at Susan's door for killing her husband since she was already in the frame for topping her lover boy.'

Ursula swung the spade and Ciaran yelled.

* * *

'Let's go home, Daddy. It's Baltic out here.'

'OK, love. I fancy a nice cup of cocoa before bed.'

'What about me?' Ciaran sobbed.

'No cocoa for you, sunshine. You have a wee think about what you've done before the cops get here,' said Sidney.

'So, you're not going to kill me?'

'Na, we were only messing with you,' said Ursula, tossing her spade into the back of the van. 'We've got it all recorded on my daddy's phone, so don't be thinking of telling a different story to the cops.

'It's been a long day, love,' said Sidney.

They climbed into the van. Sidney looked weary from the day's events.

'Daddy? Did you remember to press the wee record button on your phone?'

'I think so.'

Ursula took Sidney's mobile and quickly searched for the recording.

'Ach, Daddy!'

Chapter 57

The 8.45 BA flight from Heathrow lowered its landing gear as it swept by the window. Sidney was up bright and early. He had a busy day ahead. Ursula too. Bless her, he thought, already frying bacon, eggs, soda and potato bread. They needed a hearty breakfast.

'You remember I have my aikido class tonight?'

'OK, love. There's a wee gig at the Blues Den, I might dander down to that later.'

Sidney paused on his way to the breakfast bar and pressed a button on the landline phone for any voicemail they had missed. The first message was from Jenna Carswell to say that the book club meeting was cancelled for this month. The next six messages came from an irate DCI.

Message one: 'Valentine? Call me when you get this.'

Message two: 'You have a lot of explaining to do, Valentine. You and that gawpy daughter of yours.'

'He's not very nice, Daddy. Calling me gawpy.'

Message three: 'This Cassidy woman in Friendly Street, Valentine. Does she have a connection to the murder of Desmond Crossley? Phone me.'

Message four: 'Bloody havoc, Valentine. What the hell's going on? That pair in the Lexus are saying nothing. The family that escaped the fire mentioned a guy named Ciaran McDermott. A patrol, acting on a tip-off, came across a man by that name. He's claiming somebody tried to kill him. Uniforms found him tied to a chair on Tyrella beach. Do you know about him, Valentine?'

Message five: 'Valentine, do you reckon this McDermott bloke killed Desmond Crossley? We picked up a guy named Sean Barnes close to where that cottage was burned. Any ideas about him? He insists he knows nothing about the blokes shot in the Mournes, but he did have a gun on him. The thing is we hadn't even mentioned those killings to him. Do you think he's our man, Valentine?'

Message six: 'We need to talk. Susan Crossley, according to the Gardai in Dublin, boarded a flight to Cape Town last Saturday. What do you think, Valentine? Call me when you get this. I told you to keep your nose out. Now there are bodies all over the place. Call me, Valentine!'

'It's a brighter day than yesterday,' said Sidney, absorbing the view across the lough. 'Whenever we've finished filling in the blanks for the corporal, do you fancy a dander along the seafront?'

'It'll have to be a short one, Daddy. We have two more fraud cases just in from the DHSS.'

If you enjoyed this book, please let others know by leaving a quick review on Amazon. Also, if you spot anything untoward in the paperback, get in touch. We strive for the best quality and appreciate reader feedback.

editor@thebookfolks.com

www.thebookfolks.com

More books by Robert McCracken

THE DETECTIVE INSPECTOR
TARA GROGAN SERIES

Merseyside Police detective Tara Grogan scarcely looks old enough to be a police officer never mind a detective inspector. Maybe because of this she is more determined than most to prove herself capable when investigating murder on the streets of Liverpool. But her tendency to become emotionally involved in cases frequently places her in great danger and undermines her efforts to get on in the force.

FREE with Kindle Unlimited and available in paperback.

BOUND TO RUN

A romantic getaway in a remote Lake District cottage turns into a desperate fight for survival for Alex Chase. If she can get away from her pursuer, and that's a big if, she'll be able to concentrate on the burning question in her mind: how to get revenge.

FREE with Kindle Unlimited and available in paperback.

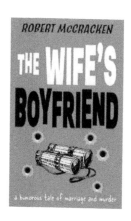

THE WIFE'S BOYFRIEND

Charlie Geddis is thrown out by his wife but, determined to win her back, decides to prove that her new boyfriend, a property developer with a lot of assets, is in fact a lying crook. In the process, he becomes embroiled in a web of bribes, infidelities and possibly a murder.

FREE with Kindle Unlimited and available in paperback.

Other titles of interest

OUT FOR REVENGE by Tony Bassett

There's a noticeable change of atmosphere in the city of Birmingham when a dangerous prisoner is released. He has plans to up his drugs business. But someone will quickly put an end to that. Detective Sunita Roy has the unenviable task of hunting down the gangsters who were likely responsible. But when the cops close in, they'll have an even bigger problem than they first imagined.

FREE with Kindle Unlimited and available in paperback.

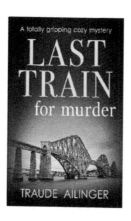

LAST TRAIN FOR MURDER by Traude Ailinger

An investigative journalist who made a career out of
sticking it to the man dies on a train to Edinburgh, having
been poisoned. DI Russell McCord struggles in the
investigation after getting banned from contacting helpful
but self-serving reporter Amy Thornton. But the latter is
ready to go in, all guns blazing. After the smoke has
cleared, what will remain standing?

FREE with Kindle Unlimited and available in paperback.

www.thebookfolks.com

Printed in Great Britain
by Amazon

37721177R00118